ANTHELION:

Love and War, Book 4

R. A. STEFFAN

INTRODUCTION

This book contains graphic violence and explicit LGBT sexual content. It is intended for a mature audience. While it is part of a series with an over-arching plot, it may be read as a standalone with a satisfying conclusion for the two main characters. If you do not intend to continue the series, you may wish to avoid the epilogue.

TABLE OF CONTENTS

ONE

Presumably, there existed a time—buried somewhere in the murky past—when Ash's life had *not* been a raging dumpster fire. It only stood to reason. He'd been a normal enough child, with a normal enough family. Friends. School. Hobbies. Days passing in a neat row without the constant, pulse-pounding sense that everything was poised to come crashing down at any moment.

Scenery slid past the tinted window of the posh hovercar that would transport him to the estate belonging to the Adjunct to the Premiere's Clandestine Operations Office. The property was located outside of the Capital—the seat of government on the colony planet of Ilarius. Ash gazed at his surroundings with unfocused eyes, trying not to think too closely about what the coming weeks would hold for him. The stiff new leather of the collar around his neck squeezed his flesh like unforgiving fingers, but he resisted the urge to tug at it.

For some time now, Ash had known that of all the members of the small vigilante resistance group that called itself the Shadow Wing, he alone held the best chance of gaining a powerful off-planet ally for their cause of overthrowing the planet's corrupt ruling party. The ragtag collection of human and Vithi would-be revolutionaries was determined to stand against the Vithii-led Regime, a xenophobic coalition that seemed intent on grinding the human population of Ilarius into the dirt. But despite a handful of small victories dragged from the jaws of defeat—usually at great cost—the last couple of months had brimmed with the sense of time running out... of walls closing in around them.

That was why Ash had decided to act.

After months of stringing along the Adjunct—a Vithii by the name of Denrir Lusivian—Ash had finally accepted his slave collar. And may all the gods and prophets have mercy on Ash's battered excuse for a soul now that he'd taken that final, irrevocable step.

As a *veelaht*—the human body-slave of a male Vithii—Ash was trading his personhood for money. At least, that was what anyone on the outside would assume. In reality, he'd traded his personhood for something else entirely. Namely, a chance to cozy up to his target in private surroundings. And that target was not, as most people might have assumed, the Adjunct himself.

It was true that as a higher-up in the Regime, Denrir had let slip some useful nuggets of information in the past. The Clandestine Operations Office was often at the leading edge of new attacks aimed at the human population—assassinations of key figures... infiltration into anti Regime groups... even the development of secret bioweapons. But the intelligence gained from the Adjunct was merely a secondary benefit, not the main objective.

No, Ash's real target was the Adjunct's bondmate, Jontalyss Lusivian. To get the access to her that he needed, Ash had just sold himself body and soul to a sadist.

Oddly enough, that wasn't even the part that had his heart racing and his palms sweating beneath the cool exterior he presented to the world. It *should* have been, to be sure… but it wasn't. The only silver lining of the situation was that Ash probably wouldn't live long enough to reap the consequences of the *other* decision he'd made in the past few days.

But he couldn't allow himself to think about any of that right now. Ash focused his attention more firmly on the scenery beyond the window, his eyes falling on a billboard for one of the more popular investment services in the Ilarian Capital. An instant later, a bark of inappropriate laughter almost choked him. He ruthlessly swallowed it down before it could escape past the constriction of the collar.

"RELAX," the sign blared in flashing neon lettering. "AND LET US WORRY ABOUT EVERYTHING."

Sure thing. I'll get right on that, he thought, the words bearing a faintly hysterical undertone within the privacy of his own mind. What a pity there wasn't a handy company he and his friends could hire to make sure that the corrupt government of Ilarius fell before it could successfully commit genocide against half the colony's population, right? It certainly would make things simpler if there were. But even back on Old Earth before the Diaspora, the humans had a saying—'If you want something done right, do it yourself.'

Or, perhaps more apropos in the current circumstances—'The only thing necessary for the triumph of evil is for good men to do nothing.' Ash had been privileged, these past few years, to dwell among a group of good men and women who knew better than to wait for someone else to step up and oppose the Regime. With his current actions, he hoped he might give his companions a better chance at surviving the coming civil war than they would otherwise have had.

For that chance, he would take whatever punishment Denrir Lusivian could dish out.

The clear barrier separating the hovercar's back seat from the driver's area lowered with a faint hum, startling him out of his reverie. *Jumpy, Ash. You'll need to keep a tight lid on that.*

The chauffeur—an elderly Vithii in a smart black suit and billed cap—met Ash's eyes in the rearview mirror. He had the two-meter frame, bronze skin, and rough-carved features common to his race, but his spiky hair was nearly white where it poked out from beneath the cap, and the passage of time seemed to have softened his sharp edges rather than honing them.

"I just wanted to inform you that there's a disturbance of some sort up ahead," he said. "It appears our arrival may be delayed."

Ash caught a glimpse of flashing lights through the front windshield, along with smoke and flames indicating a major accident of some kind.

"Thank you for letting me know," he said absently. Sometimes it could be oddly jarring to interact with Vithii who weren't xenophobic arseholes. The Adjunct's driver had been nothing but polite to Ash since picking him up, despite the leather collar advertising his status as a nonperson—as *property*—for anyone and everyone to see. If Ash had been able to feel much of anything at all these days, he probably would have felt bad that the sweet old bloke was probably going to end up dead soon.

"*What the*—?" exclaimed the sweet old bloke in question.

Instinctively, Ash braced against the front seat with both hands as the hovercar braked hard and slewed sideways, machinery screeching in protest as the stabilizers tried to kick in. He closed his eyes. The impact of metal against metal an instant later should have been shocking.

It wasn't, though. If anything, it had a distinct air of inevitability about it.

Draven paced back and forth in the cramped space between the bed and the wall in Pax's quarters. The remote stellar cartography outpost where he and the other members of the Shadow Wing were currently hunkered down might have been state-of-the-art in his grandsire's time, but now it was grungy, rusting, and in dire need of renovation.

Of course, the place was only useful to them as a safe haven because it had been abandoned years ago. It had come in handy as an offworld hideout on several occasions now—most recently, when the authorities had painted a target on Pax and his new bondmate after they attempted to infiltrate the Regime's cyborg research program.

It had been a foregone conclusion that the rest of the group would join them here, so they could jointly plan their next move in the never-ending struggle to stay one step ahead of the corrupt government on Ilarius. Well… *most* of the rest of the group, anyway.

One person was notably missing.

At any rate, after nearly two weeks cooped up on the obscure little moon, Draven was about to go mad. In some ways, he envied Pax. Since his emotion centers had long ago been excised by his Vithii military handlers, the cyborg would never have to deal with feelings of frustration, boredom, or worry—at least, not unless he was experiencing them via the mental bond he shared with his telepathic lover.

And that was another reason to envy Pax. His bondmate Nahleene was a half- Maelfian ex-diplomat with political and intelligence connections on her mother's homeworld, which meant that she and Pax had an excuse to get off this barren rock and go do something useful.

Indeed, Pax was currently engaged in packing up his meager belongings for transport, ignoring Draven's crackling aura of edginess as he prowled six steps forward and six steps back, crossing the length of the room over and over. Normally, the cyborg wouldn't have been Draven's first choice as a sounding board. There was something vaguely unsatisfying about complaining to a person who exhibited no emotional reaction whatsoever to your words.

At the moment, though, Pax was the only viable option. Hunter, Kade, and Ryder had grown so tired of listening to Draven's bitching that they basically chased him off whenever he brought up the subject of Ash. He didn't really know Nahleene well enough to discuss things with her. And the humans, Skye and Temple, got so upset about the topic that it made him feel guilty afterward.

That left Pax. And, hey, whatever else you wanted to say about him, Pax was a good listener.

"He's been out of contact for days now!" Draven said, not for the first time since he'd invited himself into the cyborg's quarters.

"Yes," Pax agreed mildly. "And there is no mystery behind his communications silence. You cannot expect Ash to be in contact during a mission such as the one he is currently undertaking with the Adjunct."

Draven paused in his pacing long enough to thump a fist against the durasteel bulkhead. Flakes of rust scraped at his skin before falling to the deckplates as lightly as snow crystals. Pax didn't even look up from his packing.

"It's a *stupid* mission," Draven growled. "No one asked him to sell his body to perverts like some kind of a cheap, street-corner *whore*!"

Now Pax paused, lifting placid, steel-blue eyes to meet Draven's amber ones. The metal implants covering the left side of the cyborg's face glinted in the overhead lighting. "'Cheap?' My understanding of such arrangements is that they are far from inexpensive for the purchaser."

"*That's not the point*!" Draven nearly shouted.

Pax regarded him curiously. "While Ash's mission may be a dangerous one, to call it stupid is facile. He is attempting to gain meaningful offworld allies willing to support the Premiere's ouster, and the dissolution of the Regime. It is the same goal Nahleene and I are pursuing, albeit by a less physically hazardous route. You are aware of these facts."

Draven clenched his jaw and spoke through gritted teeth. "Right. Because if Nahleene had suggested selling herself into slavery as a way to get offworld help, I'm sure you'd be totally fine with it!"

It was a low blow, and with anyone else on the station, it would also be a good way to get punched in the face. But Pax only tilted his head.

"May I ask a personal question, Draven? There is something I have wondered about for a long time now."

With difficulty, Draven wrestled his temper under control and turned away from that flat gaze. It was unusual for Pax to come out with anything personal. In fact, it was unusual enough that blowing off the question would have made Draven feel like an asshole. "Yeah, I guess? What did you want to ask me, Pax?"

"Why have you never simply told Ash how you feel about him?"

Draven froze, tension hardening his spine into a titanium rod. A lifetime of locking away the truth settled over him, making the recycled air catch in his lungs. The long years of hiding away the deepest parts of himself so they didn't end up getting him killed suddenly felt like a heavy, leaden cloak.

"*Excuse* me? What the hell are you trying to imply, Pax?" he snapped, wrapping belligerence around himself like a shield.

Draven silently cursed the way his heart rate sped up, knowing the cyborg had sensors trained on him that would make the involuntary reaction stand out like a giant white flag flapping in the breeze. He could only hope that Pax would interpret his physical response as anger, rather than… anything else.

"I am not implying anything," Pax said with infuriating serenity. "Merely asking a question, as I stated beforehand."

"Do you think I'm some kind of invert?" Draven demanded, falling back on the aggression that had kept him alive through an adolescence spent living on the streets in a violently homophobic Vithii culture.

The whole exchange was so unexpected that his hands began to shake, so he clenched them into fists at his hips. He felt caught between the rational part of his mind—a part that knew Pax would not suddenly turn on him after their years of friendship—and the memories of seeing young Vithii males beaten and killed simply because someone with authority had accused them of having *unnatural desires*. Draven made himself breathe slowly and evenly.

Pax—and every other Vithii on this station, for that matter—tolerated Ash's open homosexuality. But... Ash was human, and humans were different. Vithii weren't supposed to be inverts. At least, not unless they were rich and powerful enough to quietly buy themselves a human *veelaht*, and pretend that what they did to their 'property' behind closed doors was something different than what it really was.

His jaw tightened until his teeth ached.

Pax continued to watch him curiously, waiting for an answer.

"Even if I was... like that—*which I'm not*," Draven hastened to add, "everyone knows Vithii males are too dominant to couple with another male without tearing them apart. Especially a human! It's just a biological fact, right?"

Pax only raised an eyebrow. Draven resumed pacing, even as he plowed ahead.

"I mean, look what those Regime assholes do to Ash. He's smaller and weaker than they are—he can't even defend himself!" He felt his heart pounding again, thudding against his chest like a jackhammer. It took a couple of hard swallows before he could continue. "If I did have some kind of twisted… *feelings*… for Ash, I'd hardly want to drag him into something that would end up with him getting hurt, now would I? So I ask again, Pax—what the hell kind of asshole do you take me for?"

The cyborg lowered his eyebrow. "Sadism and sexual attraction are not the same thing," he said. "Since you are not a sadist, Draven, surely that does not require saying."

Draven only scoffed, wondering if Pax were being deliberately obtuse, or if his tech-enhanced brain were somehow incapable of truly understanding the issue at hand.

Still, Pax regarded him like he was some kind of mildly interesting lab experiment. "You speak of Vithii male dominance instincts," the cyborg said, "but Vithii also have free will and the ability to control their own behavior. We are not beasts."

"Some of us sure seem to *behave* like beasts," Draven muttered, thinking of every horrible act that had been perpetrated in the last twenty years under the auspices of the Vithii First movement.

"Irrelevant, since it is you in particular we are discussing," Pax insisted. "Sexual dominance means taking responsibility for the wellbeing of one's partner—nothing more, nothing less. You must surely be aware that the practice of homosexuality exists among Vithii in the Ilarian military? Not openly, perhaps, but it is there. And yet, somehow, the males manage not to tear each other apart while attempting to be the dominant partner."

Draven stared at Pax, unsure whether he was more surprised at the words coming out of the cyborg's mouth, or the fact that Nahleene's sarcasm appeared to be rubbing off on him even when the pair wasn't in direct telepathic contact. What he'd just said… couldn't be true. Could it?

"You have got to be fucking *joking*," he managed.

Pax blinked. "Why would I wish to employ a story with a humorous punch line when the subject we are discussing is a serious one?" he asked.

Draven opened his mouth to say… something. The gods alone knew what. Before he could, however, he was interrupted by the rap of knuckles against the edge of the open doorway leading into Pax's quarters. He turned to find Temple hovering in the room's entrance. The human's complexion was an unhealthy shade of gray beneath the dark brown of his skin, and something about his expression made Draven's stomach dip unpleasantly.

"Yes, Temple?" Pax asked. "You appear unwell. Do you require assistance?"

Temple swallowed, his throat bobbing visibly. His hand gripped the doorframe, and his dark eyes flitted between the two of them before fixing on a neutral spot on the floor.

"You both need to come to the control center, stat," he said. "You know Kade has been monitoring Ilarian communications and news sources for a list of keywords related to us, and to the situation in the Capital, right?"

"Yeah, of course we do," Draven said, forcing the words past the growing knot of worry trying to lodge itself at the base of his throat. "He's done that for years. What about it?"

The human took a deep breath, as though to steel himself. "I'm sorry, but… he's just come across a news item about a hovercar crash outside the city. Ashildir Purandhri is listed among the confirmed casualties."

TWO

There was a split second of confusion before Draven's frozen thoughts struggled past the unexpectedness of hearing Temple use Ash's full name. None of them ever used it. They never had. In fact, Draven would have quoted long odds that it was the name the human had been born with—not when he knew Ash had smuggled both of his parents off-planet years ago to keep them safe. Ash was way too slippery to leave a records trail that might somehow lead back to his family on Terra Nova, thereby putting them in danger.

All this flashed through his mind in the space of a skipped heartbeat, before the sense of Temple's words settled into place.

"No," he said, the word sounding oddly as though it was coming through a tunnel. "That can't be right."

A hand closed around his upper arm, and Pax's voice came from somewhere close by. "Come. We will join the others in the control center. Lead the way please, Temple."

Draven was vaguely aware of the familiar corridors blurring around him, and the sound of boots against the deckplates. The station seemed suddenly too cold. Were the blasted environmental controls on the fritz again? He blinked several times as the door to the control room appeared in front of him, much sooner than it should have. How had they gotten here so fast?

The hand on his arm fell away an instant before the door screeched open on damaged tracks that no one ever quite seemed to find the time to repair. Draven hadn't even realized that Pax was still holding onto him.

The aura of heaviness coming from inside the room hit him like a wall, nearly sending him staggering backward a step. He pushed through it, still feeling that oddly dreamlike distance wrapped around him like muffling insulation.

The place looked like the aftermath of a human funeral. His eyes fell on Skye. The blonde-haired human female was weeping silently, one hand pressed across the lower half of her face. Hunter and Kade looked grim. Ryder looked like she wanted to tear the limbs off someone. Nahleene brushed past Draven and walked into Pax's arms, murmuring words of comfort to a cyborg who could never need them. Why were all of them behaving this way?

"No," Draven said again. "This is wrong. Why are you all acting like you believe this shit?"

"Draven," Hunter began. The powerful Vithii leader's jaw tightened, making the distinctive raven-feather tattoos on his nook ripple.

"No!" Draven said again. "Kade, you tell me what you found! Don't leave anything out. There's obviously been a mistake—"

Kade scrubbed a hand through his dark spikes of hair. Draven thought the Vithii must be due for a dose of neurotonin stabilizer soon, because he looked pale and shaky—even though none of that came through in his voice.

"The report is from a government-controlled news outlet," Kade began, "but there are corroborating eyewitness reports from some of the more reliable underground media sites. Apparently, three private hovercars were involved in a fiery crash on the outskirts of the Capital with a freight transport carrying liquid fuel. All six people involved were killed—five Vithii and one human."

"That doesn't mean anything!" Draven insisted. "Ash had no reason to travel outside of the city."

"*Draven*," Hunter's tone held the full weight of command this time. "Let him finish."

Kade let out a harsh breath. "The heat of the fuel fire left the bodies in such bad condition that they had to be identified by DNA testing. The names were listed, and Ash was one of them." His mouth twisted. "A short note in the article mentions that one of the hovercars belonged to the Adjunct to the Premiere's Clandestine Operations office, but that the Adjunct himself was not involved in the accident."

The chill in Draven's stomach spread outward. *The Adjunct.* The Vithii government official Ash had been courting as a *veelaht* over the past weeks, and a man Draven would happily murder with his bare hands.

"That still doesn't make sense," he said, surprised when his voice sounded as weak and reedy as if he'd been running a marathon. "Ash wasn't supposed to let the Adjunct get him someplace isolated. He was supposed to stay in the Capital."

Pax took Draven's arm again and made as though to urge him toward a chair. Draven jerked free angrily, even though he was aware on some level that if Pax wanted to manhandle him, he'd be as helpless as a toddler against the powerful cy-borg. But he didn't need to sit down; he *needed* everyone else to stop acting like they believed this *greilo*-shit.

There was a hint of pity in Hunter's eyes that Draven really didn't like. "On the contrary," Hunter said, "he was always going to end up infiltrating the Adjunct's private residence. How else could he get the access he needed? He just wasn't supposed to do it *yet*."

Draven seized on the words. "He's been cap-tured, then. The Adjunct must have figured out what he was up to, and this is the Regime's way of making him disappear. We have to find him and get him back somehow."

Hunter's gaze met Kade's, the two communi-cating in that silent way they sometimes did. Kade's frown deepened, and he sighed. Skye had been watching them, too, and she turned to her Vithii bondmate with fragile hope threading through her human expression of shock and grief.

"Hunter? Could it be possible?" she asked.

Hunter gave Kade a final look. "I don't know. Kade, find a techworm who can hack into the rec-ords database. That way, we can at least confirm that the DNA really does belong to Ash. We'll make a decision on what to do next once we've inde-pendently checked it against a sample from here on the station."

Kade grunted agreement, but even so, Draven had an uncomfortable sense of being humored. *Managed.* He scowled.

"Maybe we should hold off on leaving for Maelfius until we have more information," Nahleene said uncertainly, looking at Pax. "Just in case we're needed here."

Pax nodded. "Agreed."

Hunter drew in a breath and nodded as well. "Thank you both. For now, though, there is nothing more to be done. It would be best if we left Kade to his task."

<hr>

The chiming of an all-comms alert interrupted Draven's pummeling of the heavy punching bag they'd hung in the station's makeshift workout room. Heart pounding with exertion, he caught the swinging bag in mid-arc, steadying it as Hunter's voice called everyone to the medical bay.

Finally.

Kade's hired techworm had taken nearly three full days to get into the government's citizen database and isolate the information they needed. *Ash would have taken less than half that much time*, Draven couldn't help thinking. Add to that an additional six cycles for Ryder to run a comparative DNA analysis with a hair sample retrieved from Ash's quarters on the station, and Draven was about to climb out of his damned skin.

He untaped his knuckles, noting distantly that there was copper-colored blood staining the white wrapping in a couple of places, and jogged toward the medbay. Sweat was streaming down his face and upper body, but the others would just have to deal with his stench. He'd face the station's shower with its increasingly alarming infestation of slimy green space mold after he heard the results.

Skye joined him, approaching from a T-junction and giving him a brief smile that looked forced. "Here's hoping for good news," she said.

Draven tried not to scowl, since he didn't want to upset Hunter's human mate any more than she already was. But, honestly, how could any news they might be about to get be construed as 'good'? Draven had already made up his mind that Ash wasn't dead, so that left the prospect that he was in Regime hands.

"Yeah, let's hope so," was all he said.

At the last junction in the corridor, Kade, Pax, and Nahleene joined them, and all five of them piled into the cramped medical room where the others waited.

"The DNA results are correct," Ryder said without preamble, running a hand angrily through her spikes of bright red hair. "One hundred percent match."

The Vithii medic sounded like she was holding onto composure by the thinnest of threads. Kade made a noise of disgust and threw the data padd he was holding against the nearest wall. The others were radiating that air of being at a funeral again, and not to put too fine a point on it, they were pissing Draven *right the fuck off.*

"Okay," he said. "So that means we can be fairly sure that Regime forces are holding him. I mean, I suppose they could have gotten a DNA sample some other way, but what would be the point? It only makes sense if they've captured him and want to make sure no one comes looking for him. Now we just need to figure out where to start searching. If they know who he is, they might be holding him someplace more secure than the prison—"

"Stop." Hunter's tone brooked no dissent, and Draven raised his eyebrows in disbelief.

"What the *fuck*, Hunter?" he asked. "We need to act, not stand around here moping like a bunch of paid mourners in a funeral procession! They could be interrogating him right now—"

Kade slapped his palm down on the console in front of him hard enough to rattle it.

"Draven," he grated. "Do you *seriously* think that Ash would be sloppy enough to let the Regime intelligence goons get anyplace near his real identity? Or that he'd wander off somewhere and let himself be picked up by security forces? The bloody man has always been slippery as a Terran eel. He's spent the better part of a decade making himself invisible."

The words chipped away at Draven's defenses, so he shut them out, baring his teeth.

"Well he's not dead, so the rest of you can sure as fuck *stop acting like he is*!" he shouted, fists clenching at his sides.

Complete silence fell over the crowded room, broken only by the hiss and beep of the station's aging systems. Draven realized that he was breathing hard, standing with his shoulders hunched forward as though he might physically attack the next person who dared tell him something he didn't want to hear. Ryder, Nahleene, and the two humans were watching him with wide eyes. Hunter and Kade wore wary expressions, while Pax appeared predictably stoic.

"Go someplace else and calm down," Hunter said after the silence started to become stifling. It wasn't a suggestion.

Draven wavered, his chest still rising and falling rapidly. Every instinct clamored for him to pummel someone until they agreed to take action, but Draven had been following Hunter and Kade's orders for a very long time. Only those long years of comradeship kept him from doing something rash.

He closed his eyes and swallowed hard. If none of the others were going to start making plans, then he needed to. And as badly as the rest of them were pissing him off right now, he'd do better making those plans in solitude.

"Fine," he snapped, and stalked out of the room. The low rumble of Hunter and Kade's voices behind him cut off as the medbay door slid shut—talking about *him*, no doubt, when they should have been talking about their next move.

There were few places in this damned outpost that offered enough room to pace properly. Draven wove through the maze of corridors until he came to the observatory that had once been used for the station's original remit of stellar cartography. The place was a dump now—lunar dust covering half of the observatory dome, while the consoles languished in disrepair.

His eyes fell on the couch he'd dragged in from the crew's rec area when they'd first arrived here, months ago. It sat under the half of the dome that was mostly clear of debris—a place for people to go when the walls started closing in on them. It was also where they'd found Pax, not so very long ago, after the cyborg nearly killed himself by using his own internal communications systems as the vector for a computer virus designed to destroy a rogue division of the Regime's cyborg research program.

And had the others just shrugged their shoulders and written Pax off as dead, when they'd found him unresponsive and in the midst of catastrophic systems failure? Of course they fucking hadn't. No more than they'd left Ryder to the tender mercies of the Ilarian prison system when she was captured during a spying mission, or abandoned Hunter to die of his injuries during the siege on the water treatment plant in the Capital.

Draven fought the urge to kick the observatory doorframe until his boot dented the durasteel.

"Lights, five percent," he said instead.

The harsh station lighting dimmed until only charcoal shadows remained. Draven walked to the center of the room and looked up. A myriad of distant stars making up the galactic arm winked down at him through the distortion of the dome. He stared at the awesome sight for a long time, trying to flog his brain into functioning in some sort of useful manner. Instead, all he could think about was how fucking angry he was.

"Godsdamn you, Ash," he muttered. "When I find you, I'll wring your scrawny human neck myself."

The scrape of a boot outside the open door alerted him to someone else's presence just before a deep voice said, "That sounds more than a little counterproductive."

Draven started in surprise, and then silently cursed himself for his jumpiness.

"Hunter," he said flatly.

The older Vithii strode onto the observation deck, his eyes sliding up to take in the view above them before returning to meet Draven's gaze in the low illumination.

"Sit down, Draven," Hunter said.

Again, something in Draven rebelled… and again, years of habit took over and he flopped down on the dusty couch as he'd been ordered.

"You're not going to talk me into believing he's dead," he said, just to get that out of the way.

Hunter regarded him steadily for the space of several heartbeats. "All right. In that case, let's talk about where that leaves us. Because from where I'm standing, it still leaves us right in the shit."

THREE

Draven gritted his teeth. "Every cycle we spend sitting here with our thumbs up our asses is another cycle when the Ilarian security forces could be interrogating Ash," he said. "The blasted man knows everything about our operation, Hunter. *Everything.* You can't be proposing that we just shrug and let the goons get on with their torture. They have drugs. Machines. How long do you think it'll be before they pry the location of this outpost out of him?"

Hunter crossed his arms. "If you're right and he's still alive, then we must assume that this station's location is compromised, along with Kade's business holdings, and, by extension, most of our remaining financial assets." He paused, still looking down at Draven without blinking. "Or… Ash might just be dead."

Draven glared up. "*He's. Not. Dead.*"

Hunter didn't back down. "No? Convince me that he isn't, in that case."

Draven took a deep breath, knowing he needed to keep a lid on his temper if Hunter was actually willing to hear him out. This might be his best chance to get the others moving, and his own need to *act* felt like it was in danger of strangling him.

"Kade's the one who said Ash was too slippery to ever let Regime forces get close to his real identity," he said. "So ask yourself, Hunter, how they were able to match the DNA from a random accident victim to the name he uses for his business dealings and legitimate records."

Hunter seemed to consider that for a few moments. Then he gave a brief nod, the movement so small that it was barely visible in the low light. "Agreed. That *is* an anomaly, even if it's far from incontrovertible proof. Now—tell me what, precisely, you're proposing that we do about it."

Frustration boiling over, Draven exploded to his feet and started pacing. "What do you *think* I'm proposing? We need to find him and get him out! *Haven't I already said that*?"

Hunter's continued calm made him want to hit something.

"That's not a plan, Draven. That's a wish," said the leader. "Where do you suggest we look? How do you propose we find someone who may or may not be alive... who may or may not be in Regime custody..."

"We have to do *something*!" Draven shouted, rounding on him.

Still, Hunter did not rise to his expression of temper.

"We can't just go blindly flailing around on Ilarius, in hopes that Ash is still alive and we might miraculously stumble across him." The words were level, and they held a note of finality. "That would be the fastest way to end up with more of our members captured for interrogation and execution."

"But—"

Hunter cut him off. "I'm sorry, Draven." His chest rose and fell heavily. "The rest of us cared for him, too—but the mission to gain offworld support against the Regime is at a critical stage, and it has to take precedence. No matter what."

Hunter could have punched Draven in the gut, and it would have been less painful than hearing those words coming out of his mouth. The words he was about to utter in reply hurt almost as much.

"Ash *was* the mission," Draven whispered.

"Ash was *part* of the mission," Hunter retorted. "We still have Pax and Nahleene. It's more important than ever now that they reach out to the authorities on Maelfius. They're our last remaining chance at gaining meaningful help against the Premiere's government."

Draven started pacing again. "It won't be enough. Maelfius isn't a military power."

"Maelfius is what we have left," Hunter said, his tone inexorable. "I've ordered the two of them to prep my fighter and leave as soon as possible."

"This whole thing is fucked, Hunter," Draven growled.

"Yes," Hunter said, compassion coloring the word. "It is. It's war, Draven… or it soon will be."

Nahleene and Pax embarked from the station the following morning, leaving the remaining six members of the Shadow Wing with Kade's two-seat fighter and a stolen transport ship Ash had liberated from the Capital after his hopper's systems had been fried during a security raid.

Draven spent the next day arguing himself hoarse to anyone who would listen.

"Come on, Kade," he said, ignoring the dark aura of *go-away* vibes that seemed to surround the older Vithii like a storm cloud. "*Listen* to me. You have to see how important this is."

"I see how suicidal it is," Kade replied, his voice flat. "Does that count?"

"It's an obvious setup," Draven argued. "He wouldn't have left the Capital without giving us a heads-up first, warning us that he was going in deeper."

Kade looked up from the data he was poring over, disbelief in his steel gray gaze. "Are you joking? Of course he fucking would. The bastard had a martyr complex the size of this moon. He went off-script, and got himself killed for his trouble."

"He's not dead."

The look of disbelief turned jaded. "Draven. Emergency services pulled his charred body out of a melted hovercar. Look. I'm sorry your friend—or whatever you want to call him—is gone. Now stop trying to wheedle me into going against Hunter's orders so you can get yourself killed, too, on the strength of a damned *hunch*. I am very much not in the mood right now."

Things didn't go any better with Ryder. If anything, they went worse.

"I miss him, too," said the medic. "Even if I wanted to shake him until his teeth rattled most of the time."

Ryder was clearly taking the whole thing hard, and Draven had hoped that might mean she'd be more receptive to his arguments. Instead, she still sounded like she might burst into Vithii funerary howls at any moment—and that wasn't what he needed from her right now. It wasn't what he needed from any of them, damn it.

"I don't *miss* him," he snapped. "I want to *save* him. I want… *us*… to save him."

"How?" Ryder snapped right back at him. "Tell me where you think we should go and what you think we should do to find someone who is most likely dead—and if not dead, then locked away in the deepest, darkest hole that the Regime sadists can come up with?"

Her scent soured with anger and frustration as she spoke, but Draven was pissed off and frustrated, too.

"So we should just give up on him?" he flung at her. "You think that's the right thing—the *honorable* thing—to do, Ryder? I didn't hear you complaining when the rest of us risked our lives to pull you out of the Regime's hands not so long ago!"

It was a step too far, and he knew it. Ryder went very still, the blood draining from her bronze Vithii complexion.

"Get out," she said in a monotone. "*Now*. I don't want to see you in this sickbay again unless you're spurting blood from a major artery."

Even though he was shaking with suppressed rage at the unfairness of it all, on some level Draven knew he should apologize for what he'd just said. He didn't. Instead, he turned and stalked out of the medical bay with a sharp curse, letting the door snap shut behind him.

As it turned out, he didn't have to go looking for the next person on his list. Temple—Ryder's human lover—found *him*. Draven was in the canteen, forcing himself to gulp down a reconstituted Redi-Meal since he knew he'd need to keep his strength up for whatever rescue mission he eventually managed to mount. Temple came in, pulled out a chair directly across from him, and lowered himself into it.

Draven stopped eating and regarded the dark-skinned human. Temple sighed and ran a hand through his short dreadlocks before catching and holding Draven's eyes with his dark ones.

"Look," he said. "You're Vithii, and I'm human, and you could snap me in half like a twig if you wanted to, *blah, blah, blah*. But you have to know you can't shit all over Ryder like that, and not expect me to come here afterward to tell you to stop being an ass. So… stop being an ass."

Draven didn't look away. "Well done. You've discharged your duty as Ryder's lover—though you might want to brush up on your threats, because they really need some serious work. Now, tell me something. Are you honestly more upset over Ryder's hurt feelings than you are over the fact that Ash could be undergoing interrogation and torture while we're sitting here talking about etiquette?"

Temple's mouth flattened into a thin line. "I'm capable of being upset about both things at the same time, thanks. Though the part you don't seem to want to hear is that the news report could be exactly what it looks like—an accounting of a tragic accident that killed a bunch of people, including a guy that all of us here care about."

"It's not."

Temple kept talking as if he hadn't spoken. "And having you go crashing around on Ilarius asking the wrong questions of the wrong people sounds like a damned good way to make sure that we end up mourning two deaths rather than one."

"*It's not.*"

They continued to stare each other down, the seconds ticking by.

Temple pushed away from the table and stood. "You and I aren't terribly close, Draven. But take a bit of free advice, will you? Whatever you're trying to accomplish here, pissing off your allies isn't the way to do it."

He left, the canteen door screeching along its rusty tracks. Draven stared after him for a long moment before turning his attention back to the congealed remains of his Redi-Meal.

———◆———

He had a surprisingly difficult time running Skye to ground. As upset as she'd been, Draven had expected her to remain close to Hunter's side, which would admittedly have presented a logistical challenge when it came to speaking with her privately. But there was no sign of her in the main part of the station, so he went looking for her elsewhere.

He finally found her in a deserted section of corridor near the generator room, engaged in target practice with a laser pistol set on low to avoid any chance of structural damage to the walls. Draven hung back, trying to gauge her mood by watching her make a round of shots at a plastic target she'd set up at the next T-junction.

While the human was a tough example of her species in many ways, she was also by far the most openly emotional person on the station. In addition to a perfectly natural desire not to upset the mate of the station's dominant male, Draven also found that seeing her blatantly express grief made him physically ache with the need to comfort her. Maybe—as a Vithii male—that reaction was hardwired into his genetics, even in someone like him whose character was twisted into unnatural shapes in other ways.

So, he watched from a distance for a few minutes as Skye methodically burned the center out of the target's hand-drawn concentric rings, her spine rigid and her stance unbending. When she lowered the pistol, he cleared his throat, not wanting to startle her when she was armed.

She whirled, and he was surprised to see that she'd apparently been shooting bullseyes through a film of tears—enough of them that some had overflowed to form twin trails down her pale cheeks.

"Draven," she said, her voice emerging steadily enough, if a bit hoarse. "Hey. How are you doing? Sorry I disappeared on you all. Does someone need me for something?"

He ignored the question about his wellbeing, since it was irrelevant. "No, nothing's going on. I just wanted to talk to you privately."

She gestured around the deserted surroundings before swiping at her eyes and holstering the compact weapon in her belt. "Talk away."

He crossed his arms and leaned against the wall of the corridor, while she mirrored him on the other side.

"I'm going after Ash," he said without preamble.

She shivered, hugging herself. "Do you really think he could still be alive?"

Draven's shoulders were so tense they ached. "He has to be."

And... *shit*. That wasn't what he'd meant to say.

"I mean," he hurried on, "it would explain how the security forces were able to connect his DNA results to his official records. You know him, Skye. You think Ash wouldn't have attached fake genetics records to his official file?"

The human blinked large blue eyes, a stirring of hope visible in her expression. "Damn. Draven—you're right. He never overlooked things like that, did he?"

"No. He didn't."

She swallowed. "I'm guessing the fact that you're talking to me about this means you've already tried Hunter, and he shot you down because what you're proposing is too risky."

No one had ever accused Skye of being slow on the uptake.

"Hunter, Kade, Ryder, and Temple, yeah," he admitted. "They're not thinking clearly about this, Skye. I need you to talk to Hunter. Get him to see that we can't just sit here and do nothing."

Her eyebrows went up. "You want me to somehow talk Hunter into risking more people when he believes he's just let one man go to his death, and sent two more on a dangerous mission with no backup?"

"… Yes?" Draven said.

Skye shook her head in disbelief. "I'm his bondmate, Draven. Not a miracle worker. You should have caught Nahleene before she left if you wanted someone with mind-control powers."

"I tried," Draven muttered. "She refused."

Skye looked like she was battling herself. Her teeth caught at her full lower lip, rolling it as she stared at a section of corridor wall next to Draven's left shoulder. He resisted the urge to immediately press her further, since she was the first person who'd really *listened* to what he was saying.

After a long pause, she straightened her spine and met his gaze directly.

"I still remember when Hunter was injured during the battle at the water treatment plant, and Kade teleported me to the safehouse where Ash was waiting," she began. "I begged Ash to send me back... to save Hunter instead. He refused."

Draven waited for her to continue. The part he remembered most from that day was what had happened *after* the battle. He'd stayed behind after the others had evacuated, intending to destroy the matter transport pad so that the Regime's security forces couldn't use it to follow them through to the safehouse.

But once the others were safe, Ash had teleported to the battle site to take his place. The human had tricked him into transporting to safety so that Draven—as a Vithii—wouldn't be stuck trying to make his way on foot through what had, by that time, devolved into a city-wide riot by the Capital's human population.

"Hunter won't budge on his decision," Skye continued, dragging Draven back to the present. "You already know that. But if you promise me one thing first, I'll help you get back to Ilarius myself."

The cynical part of Draven—which was a pretty fucking *large* part, these days—wondered what, exactly, Skye thought she'd be able to do to help him. He quashed the knee-jerk response, however—because the human had already accomplished things that no one would think she'd be capable of.

"What kind of promise?" he asked instead.

She surprised him by crossing the corridor and taking his hands in her delicate human ones. "Promise me that Ash really is alive, and I'm not just helping you commit suicide by doing something idiotic and self-destructive."

Draven blinked down at her. It would be so easy. *Sure, Skye—I promise. You know I'm not the suicidal type.* He was a consummate liar—after all, he'd spent most of his life lying about things. But somehow, he just couldn't bring himself to do it here and now. Not to her.

He squeezed her hands, being careful not to use too much force. "I can't tell you what you want me to tell you. But I'm getting Ash back, Skye. No matter what. That much I swear."

Her cut-crystal gaze bored into him. "And if he really is dead?" she asked, her voice thick.

For the first time, Draven felt the possibility settle into his bones in a tangible way, cold radiating outward from the marrow. His own voice was suspiciously raspy when he replied, "Then I'm still getting him back."

Because he would never truly believe it unless he saw the evidence with his own eyes. Until Ryder ran a DNA sample from the corpse against their real sample and told him to his face that it was a match, Ash was alive.

Period.

FOUR

Skye showed up at his quarters a few cycles later in the station's evening.

"I told Hunter that Kade and I were going to take his fighter out for a cycle or two so that I could get a better feel for the controls," she told him. "Then I told Kade that it was Hunter I'd be going with. If either of them think to double-check my story, we're screwed—so don't dawdle."

Draven raised an eyebrow, looking her up and down. She was dressed in a black flightsuit, her hair pulled back in a tight knot, a small carryall slung over her shoulder.

"Remind me not to underestimate you," he said, throwing a few more weapons and supplies into his duffel. "You've obviously been hiding a devious streak none of us knew about."

"Not really," she said, motioning him to follow her toward the station's secondary umbilical port. "I'm just tired of standing around while the Premiere destroys everyone and everything I give a shit about."

The outpost had already switched over to night mode, the lights dimming until shadows lurked around every bend. As Skye had said, it would just take one person asking the wrong question or strolling through the wrong part of the station for her hastily conceived plan to fall apart. On the positive side, with Pax gone, no one would be constantly monitoring the movement of their life signs through the outpost. His and Nahleene's absence also meant there were fewer people they might run into.

Unfortunately, that didn't stop fate from sticking its nose in. They rounded the last corner and ran straight into Temple coming from the direction of the primary umbilical, where the stolen transport was docked.

"*Damn it*," Skye muttered under her breath, the words barely audible.

"Skye?" Temple asked, his eyes taking in her flightsuit, as well as Draven's presence behind her shoulder. "What are you doing here?"

Skye stopped a few paces in front of her foster brother. "Back at you, big brother—what are *you* doing here?"

Temple shrugged. "The readings from the transport's coolant system were acting wonky earlier. I was patching the leak, since we can't exactly afford to lose a ship now that we're down to two. Now—your turn."

"Hunter wanted me to get a feel for Kade's fighter," she said with admirable poise. "I've trained on Hunter's ship before, but since Nahleene and Pax took it, we figured I ought to log some cycles on Kade's while things were relatively quiet. He was going to take me up himself, but something came up, so Draven offered to do it."

She was good. Good enough that Draven thought she might get away with the lie at first. But he'd underestimated the familiarity of two people who'd grown up together as children. Temple glanced over Draven's bulging duffel bag and raised an eyebrow, before turning a look on Skye that clearly screamed *bullshit.*

"Uh-huh," he said. "Sure. Or else you're smuggling Draven back to Ilarius so he can get himself killed looking for someone who may or may not even be alive."

Draven readied himself, trying to decide if he could restrain Temple or render him unconscious without risking doing him any serious damage... and if Skye would still agree to help him if he did so.

"Yes," Skye said, surprising him. "Or possibly that."

Temple sighed explosively. "*Prophets*, little sis. Have I taught you *nothing*? You're supposed to play dumb so I can maintain my shield of plausible deniability."

But Skye shook her head. "Cut the crap. We both know Draven has to do this, but we can't afford to lose our access to Kade's fighter if he goes to Ilarius alone. I'll drop him off and come back right afterward. Temple... the heat's on me for this one, okay? Just walk away and pretend you never saw us."

Temple gave Draven a long, hard look... and sighed again. He stepped up to Skye and took her shoulders in his hands, leaning down to press a kiss to her forehead.

"I hate everything about this," he said conversationally, once he'd pulled back. "Just so you know. Don't get killed, please? And if you do, be aware that I'll be right behind you, since Hunter will gut me like a fish when he figures out that I knew what you were planning."

Skye gave him a quick, tight hug and backed away. "Thanks, big bro. I'll be careful."

His lips twisted downward. "Do that." Then his eyes fell on Draven. "And *you*. I'm not even gonna waste the station's oxygen by telling you to be careful. Just… *please be right about this*. Okay?"

Draven gave a single, tight nod. Temple shot them both a final, unhappy look and continued toward the station's habitation wing, shaking his head as he left.

"Come on," Skye said. "The chrono's ticking."

◆

A few cycles later, Skye maneuvered the two-seat fighter into a temporary refueling berth inside one of Kade's less heavily frequented hangar bays in the Ilarian Capital. It was, Draven realized, the same one where they'd sheltered when returning to the planet after rescuing Skye from her crashed ship on the lunar outpost's moon.

The human double-checked her readings and started powering everything down. "Good little fighter, this," she said. "The throttle's touchier than on Hunter's ship, though."

Draven nodded, impressed by her piloting. It was easy to underestimate someone's flying skills when your first meeting with her occurred right after she'd been pulled from a pile of burning wreckage. But, in Skye's defense, there had been extenuating circumstances surrounding the crash—namely, the fact that other people had been shooting at her, and that the shuttle she'd stolen had been practically derelict to start with.

"Kade claims he prefers it that way," he said, unclipping his flight harness. "Don't stick around here too long, all right? Get back to the others, and remember to wipe the fighter's ID codes and install the new ones before you pass through the security perimeter on your way out."

"I know," she said. "I'll only stay long enough to top up the solid fuel supply. Perks of stealing the hangar owner's ship, right? Your first refueling is free."

Draven stood up in the cramped cockpit and hefted his bag. "Yeah, I guess. And, Skye? Thanks for the ride."

She waved the words away. "Like Temple said, just be right about this, Draven. Don't make me live with the guilt of a bad decision for the rest of my—probably very short—life."

"I'll find him," Draven vowed. He started to turn—then paused, debating whether to say the next words. But the way he'd left things with the others on the station finally tipped the scales. "Only… if something does happen, do one more thing for me? Tell the others… the Shadow Wing was always my family. Only one I ever had, really. And tell Ryder I'm sorry. She'll know for what."

"Hey. Now you're talking like someone who doesn't think they're coming back," Skye said. "Stop it. Get out of here and go find our friend, before I realize what a gods-awful idea this was and change my mind."

Draven snorted. "Yeah, okay. Have fun getting strips torn out of your hide by the others when you get back to the station. Oh, and I won't be reachable directly, but you know that human kid, Jonah, from the prison? You can use him as a contact for emergencies. Kade and Temple know how to reach him. I'll check in with him as I'm able."

"Will do," Skye said. "Be careful, Draven. And give Ash a hug for me if—*when*—you find him." She paused. "Maybe a smack, as well… but only if he's not too battered already."

That last part was way too dangerous to touch, so Draven only nodded and threw Skye an ironic little salute before climbing down the cockpit ladder and dropping to the hangar's plasticrete floor. He took a deep breath of the exhaust-laden planetside air, oriented himself, and headed for the staff entrance at the back of the building. He knew the security cameras there would all be doctored, playing old video on a continuous loop.

No point in making things any easier for the Capital security forces than he had to.

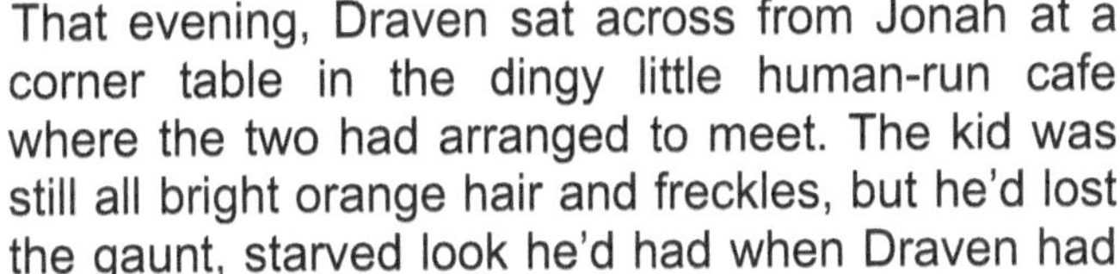

That evening, Draven sat across from Jonah at a corner table in the dingy little human-run cafe where the two had arranged to meet. The kid was still all bright orange hair and freckles, but he'd lost the gaunt, starved look he'd had when Draven had first stumbled across him while they were rescuing Ryder from Regime custody, weeks ago.

He'd be surprised if Jonah were much older than seventeen, but the boy had proven to have a good head on his shoulders, and after the mess at the prison, he also regarded Draven and the others with something akin to hero worship. Kade and Ash had provided the kid with a new identity as a way to help him get free of the gang lifestyle he'd been sucked into at an early age, and in return, Jonah seemed almost desperately eager to help them in any way he could.

"You still staying with your aunt and uncle, then?" Draven asked.

Jonah nodded. "Yeah. I managed to land a gig doing tech support for one of the big fiber optic companies, though—so I'm hoping to move out on my own in a couple of months. I don't want to do anything that might put my family members on the Regime's radar, but as long as you and the others contact me on my private comm using secure encryption, it's all good."

"Smart kid," Draven approved. "You want to make sure you defrag the comm's memory every time you delete a message, and don't leave a written record of *anything*. Just keep all of it up here." He tapped his temple for emphasis.

"I know—you don't have to worry." Jonah's reddish-brown brows drew together. "You really think he's still alive, then?"

Draven was getting incredibly tired of hearing that question after only a handful of days. "Yes," was all he said.

The kid's mouth twitched into a worried frown. "But how will you even know where to start looking?" he asked. "I mean, at least with Ryder, you already knew she was being held in the prison. *He* could be anywhere."

"I have some ideas on where to begin asking questions," Draven said grimly. "So, look—I'm not going to be able to check in on any kind of a regular schedule. When I have news and I can get it to you safely, I will. But I expect you'll get bombarded by messages from the others the moment Skye gets back to the station… 'Where is he,' 'What's he doing,' and so forth. Just delete them and forget about it if they don't contain anything important or useful. They're not pissed off at you, they're pissed off at me."

Jonah nodded, his expression sober. "I hear you. And I get why they're upset. I mean—it kind of freaks me out to see you and the others splitting up when it comes to something like this, instead of all working together. But... I really hope you find him, Draven."

Draven stood and threw a few credits on the table to cover both of their meals. He slapped Jonah on the shoulder as he headed toward the door. "Me too, kid," he threw over his shoulder. "I'll be in touch."

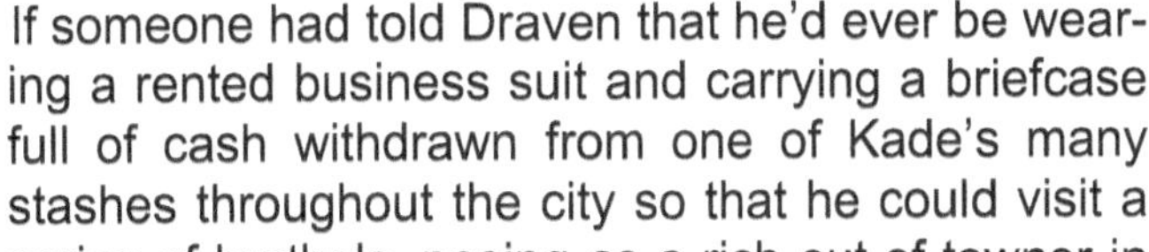

If someone had told Draven that he'd ever be wearing a rented business suit and carrying a briefcase full of cash withdrawn from one of Kade's many stashes throughout the city so that he could visit a series of brothels, posing as a rich out-of-towner in the market for a human sex slave, he would have laughed in their face.

Okay, that was actually a lie. He would have *punched* them in their face.

"I'm after one that's tall," he said to the bored-looking Vithii woman behind the counter. "But not too tall. And, uh, slender... but not too slender. I like the ones with light brownish skin and dark eyes best. And... hair."

The attendant looked up from her padd, raising an eyebrow. "Hair?" she echoed.

Draven tried not to let the fact that he currently wanted to shrivel up and disappear into the ground show openly. "Yes. Hair. Dark and straight. And, um, long. Past the shoulders, at least. Do you have anyone like that?"

Prophets... *please* let this woman be accustomed to potential clients stammering and blushing like idiots. He gritted his teeth, desperately wishing for something smooth and hard to bang his head against.

"And it has to be a male?" she asked skeptically.

Draven stumbled over a reply, every instinct screaming at him not to admit in public that, yes, it did have to be a male.

"Well... I mean... I suppose I could—"

The attendant set her padd down and sighed. "Look, sir. This establishment is very discreet. We only care about your credits, nothing else. It's my job to help you find the right match for your... recreational pursuits. I can't do that unless you tell me what it is you're after."

"Yes," Draven blurted. "It has to be a male."

She nodded briskly, the picture of professionalism. "Very well. We have several specimens that exhibit at least some of those traits—"

Draven cut her off. "I need all of them."

The woman drew breath to speak, but held it for a moment as though choosing her words. "Sir," she said delicately, "I'm sure you understand that *veelahts* are in somewhat short supply. It takes, shall we say, a rather particular type of human to agree to such an arrangement, even given generous financial compensation—and those that do tend to have a waiting list of potential clients."

A rather particular type of human.

Draven swallowed against the sensation of a steel band trying to tighten around his lungs. The sudden, irrational urge to run out the door, invent a fucking time machine, go back in time, and shake Ash until he agreed never to come within a light year of a place like this nearly overwhelmed him.

"I need a *veelaht* with all of those traits," he managed, trying his best to look stern and imposing instead of like he wanted to flee screaming from the building.

The attendant's mouth ticked down as she scrolled through screens on her padd, a furrow of concentration marring her heavy brow.

"Well… I do have one relatively recent addition that meets almost all of your criteria," she said. "All except the long hair, really. It's possible that for an extra fee, he would be willing to grow it out or get extensions—"

"Let me see," he said, cutting her off. The *recent addition* part wasn't promising, but someone's hair could be cut.

She unfolded the padd screen to its full size and slid it across to him. Draven held his breath, taking in the photo of a human male—naked except for a studded leather collar—with his body draped artfully over an oddly shaped piece of furniture like a couch with no backrest. His pulse jumped at the superficial resemblance to Ash… but it wasn't him. He slid the padd back to the attendant.

"I'll keep this one in mind as a possibility," he said, pleased at how steady his voice emerged. "But for now, I'd prefer to shop around some more in hopes of finding exactly what I want."

The attendant shrugged, clearly dismissing him from her mind now that it was obvious that no credits would be changing hands today. "As you like, sir. I'm sorry we were unable to accommodate you at the present time."

Draven gave a single, terse nod and left, already plotting the most efficient route to the next brothel. *One down, eight more to go.*

FIVE

There were very good reasons why Ash had not shared the location of the brothel where he operated with the rest of them. Draven knew this. It was the same reason he had no idea what route Pax and Nahleene were taking to Maelfius. The same reason he only knew a couple of Kade's bank account numbers, rather than all of them.

Any of them, at any time, could be captured and interrogated about other members of the Shadow Wing. When possible, it made sense not to disseminate unnecessary details related to important missions. Ash had deemed his quest to entrap the Adjunct to be such a mission, and Hunter had agreed.

That fact sure as hell wasn't making Draven's job any easier now, though.

There was only one more place to try before he'd be forced to start poking his nose into Jago's gang territory. After that, things had the potential to get very messy, very quickly. The Vithii crime boss already hated Kade and Hunter's guts, and that had been *before* Kade tricked him into renting them a drug lab for the purpose of manufacturing an antidote for the Premiere's human-specific bioweapon.

The kind of heat that had come down on Jago when the security forces traced the Shadow Wing's subversive activity back to Jago's doorstep would have cost the gang leader millions to bribe his way out of, at the very least. For that reason, Draven was hoping Ash wouldn't have been stupid enough to set foot inside one of Jago's brothels. Unfortunately, a nagging part of him kept whispering that doing so was *exactly* the kind of shit Ash would pull, because it was so unexpected.

'Who'd think to look for me in a brothel owned by someone who hates us that much?'

Draven could almost picture him saying it, punctuating the words with an airy wave and one of those bright, sharp smiles that never seemed to reach his eyes. He took a cleansing breath and let the bouncer of this latest place pat him down for weapons. Then he opened the briefcase to let the goon examine the neatly stacked credits, gleaming in the overhead lights.

"Go on," the bouncer grunted. "Main office is the first door on the left."

Draven entered the first door on the left, revealing a space divided into two very distinct halves. The place was old school, to put it mildly. There was the front half, with comfortable couches and elegant carpeting, where clients could presumably examine the merchandise up close. Then, there was the back half, crammed full of freaking *paper file cabinets*, if you could even believe such a thing.

Interesting.

There were a limited number of reasons why a business like this might choose to eschew e-records. The most obvious one was that they dealt with a clientele who didn't want any trace of electronic records linking them to a brothel. Draven's eyes slid over the metal cabinets, taking in the suspicious wiring snaking around and through them.

He'd put money on those wires being part of a failsafe system that would incinerate every document in the room at the press of a button. His heart rate picked up. This, he thought, was the kind of place where a high-up government type might feel comfortable coming. Someone like a highly placed Regime official. Like an *Adjunct*, for instance.

Draven cleared his throat, getting the attention of the elderly Vithii man puttering in the back of the office, poring over paper files. The man looked up sharply, then immediately pasted on a polite *customer service* expression.

"Hello, sir!" he began, his eyes taking in the heavy briefcase with a calculating glance. "How may I be of assistance to you on this fine day?"

Practice had so far made no impact on Draven's crawling sense of horror at what he was doing, but he gamely ran through his spiel of looking for a *veelaht* particularly suited to his refined tastes. He caught a flash of disappointment in the other Vithii's gaze after he'd finished his list of attributes that perfectly described Ash, and braced himself for another polite brush-off.

But the proprietor shook his head ruefully. "I'm afraid you're a week or so too late, sir," he said in a wry tone. "I had merchandise that would have suited you admirably, but I fear someone else already snapped him up on a permanent basis."

Draven tried to ignore his pounding heart as he asked, "Oh? Who snapped him up? Perhaps they'd be willing to sell him on to me at a profit."

He thought he'd managed to keep his tone casual, but the man's expression closed off abruptly. "Our client information is strictly confidential, sir. I'm sure you understand."

Draven backtracked quickly. "Yes, of course. My apologies—I'm new to all of this." He lifted the briefcase onto the counter and thumbed open the locks, as though trying to impress the proprietor with his ability to pay.

"I hope we can still do business," he continued, rummaging beneath the top layer of credits and pulling out the compact stunner he'd stashed there. Before the other man could do more than draw breath to call out for help, Draven shot him squarely in the chest. He crumpled to the floor, out of sight behind the counter.

After a quick visual sweep of the office walls and ceiling revealed that the inevitable security cameras must be well hidden, Draven hopped over the counter and made a circuit of the back room. He was relieved to find the control panel for the various video surveillance feeds nestled in a corner. While that was no guarantee that the feeds weren't also piped to a separate security station, it did mean he could pull up the last few minutes of footage and delete it, erasing the record of his arrival.

The punters who used this place are a bunch of idiots, he thought. *Worried about electronic payment records when the owners probably have vaults full of digital recordings showing them fucking prostitutes*

An unpleasant chill went through him at the sudden realization that he might find tape documenting Ash's abuse at the hands of the Adjunct— and who knew how many other Vithii perverts—in this very room. The idea of seeing it firsthand brought a sick feeling to his stomach, and yet it was also strangely compelling.

He shook his head sharply. That wasn't why he was here. Seeing Ash being beaten and fucked might be useful for rousing Draven into a murderous rage, but it wasn't useful for finding him. For that, he needed a different form of record.

Someone else already snapped him up on a permanent basis, the proprietor had said. And somewhere in these filing cabinets, the details of that transaction lay hidden inside a manila folder. Draven examined the locking system on the nearest cabinet, and then went to make a copy of the proprietor's thumbprint with the little black market device he'd brought along for just such a purpose.

◆

Less than half a cycle later, Draven made his way out of the employee entrance at the back, stunning the guard who was watching the door before the man even had a chance to react. He'd also disabled the security system right before leaving the office area, but it was still possible that someone in the building could have captured his presence on camera at some point.

It was a calculated risk.

In addition to the piles of credits and other clandestine odds and ends useful for a break-in, Draven's briefcase now held every paper file he'd been able to find on Ashildir Purandhri's stint as a *veelaht*-for-hire in this nameless backstreet brothel. He hadn't tried to read through them yet—he'd just grabbed everything that looked relevant and scarpered.

After that, it was simply a matter of disappearing into the city's underbelly. He could have gone to one of Kade's safehouses, but the possibility still existed that they were compromised. Rather than worrying about Regime lackeys breaking down the door unexpectedly, he went to an old bolthole he'd maintained from his early days with the street gangs. It wasn't anywhere near as posh as Kade's places, but it also wouldn't be on anybody's radar.

The old electrical substation in the undercity had never been intended for Vithii or human habitation, but it had access to power and hypernet cables, as well as a locking door. Once he'd confirmed that there were no technicians around and that no squatters had moved in, he locked the door behind him and checked the stash of essentials he'd hidden in a gap in the wall where a transformer had once been housed.

When he had a light and a small heating unit set up to combat the clammy chill of the place, he spread the files out on the floor in front of him and started reading. There was a fair amount of material to cover—everything from records of Ash's periodic sexual health testing to lists of past clients.

There was only one client in particular that interested Draven, though—the only client Ash would ever have agreed to sell himself to on a permanent basis. The moment the Vithii at the brothel had let slip that he'd done so, Draven had felt his blood pressure start to rise. Ash was supposed to let the rest of them know if and when he took that step… but he hadn't. The proof was laid out in Draven's hands now, printed in stark black and white.

Date—slightly less than a week ago. Purchaser—D. Lusivian. Purchase price—two hundred seventy-five thousand credits. A small fortune for most people on Ilarius. That kind of money would buy a respectable house in a well-to-do part of the Capital, or purchase a couple of tickets off-planet to someplace like Terra Nova or Vithara, with enough left over for any necessary bribes to get around the current Ilarian travel restrictions.

These days, it would apparently also buy a male human slave—making it the price of someone's personhood.

With a growing feeling of illness, Draven traced the money trail from Denrir Lusivian, to the brothel, and from there to an account that Draven happened to know belonged to Ash. He knew that because Ash had given him the access codes a couple of years ago, for use in emergencies.

Draven pulled out the ancient terminal he kept stashed in this place and hooked it into the hijacked hypernet access cable. The bank login codes Ash had shared with him still worked, and he was able to access the account records to show a large deposit dropping the day after the date of the brothel's purchase documents. On that same day, the funds were transferred to an offworld account on Terra Nova—one Draven wasn't familiar with.

Ash's parents, if he had to guess.

He logged out and powered the terminal down, then sat cross-legged on the floor, thinking hard. If Lusivian had decided to turn Ash over to the Regime, he wouldn't have bothered paying that kind of money to buy him first. He just would have called in some of his buddies in security and had him hauled away.

Everything about the paperwork and banking records pointed to this being a simple sale for the sale's sake. This had been Ash's intention all along, but Draven felt his anger growing at the realization that rather than stick to the plan as originally out-lined, the fucking bastard had dumped the rest of them in favor of going it completely alone.

In some ways, the action was so godsdamned predictable that Draven wanted to roar with frustration.

But one question still remained unanswered. Had Ash done this stupid, idiotic thing and then randomly been killed in a hovercar accident while on the way to his new owner's property, or had he done this stupid, idiotic thing and then further compounded his idiocy by staging his own death, in some misguided attempt to throw the rest of them off his trail?

As it had from the beginning, something deep inside Draven rebelled at the idea of Ash being dead. And either way, his only possible next step was to dig up the location of the Adjunct's private compound on the outskirts of the Capital and go there. If Ash was alive, Draven would find him and get him back, hopefully with Ash's original target in tow, as well. If Ash was dead, Draven would make sure that Denrir Lusivian died, too. Preferably after Draven had paid him back in kind for every single mark he'd ever put on Ash's body.

Draven didn't think he'd ever burned with as much anger in his life as he did at that moment. Usually, anger made him feel as though something was heating him from the inside out, but this was different. It burned cold, like liquid nitrogen.

Some of it was directed at Ash himself. Some was directed at Denrir Lusivian, the Adjunct to the Regime's Clandestine Operations Office. Some was directed at the Premiere, who'd brought all of them to this state with his hate-filled lust for power.

But a great big fucking chunk of Draven's cold rage was directed squarely at himself. Could he have somehow stopped this before it ever got this far? What if, instead of sniping and growling at Ash for constantly putting himself in the path of dangerous perverts, Draven had taken him by the shoulders, looked him in the eye, and begged him not to sell his body in exchange for secrets?

What if Draven had leaned down and pressed his lips against Ash's neck, told the human exactly how he felt, and buried his teeth in that smooth flesh to prove he was serious about his desire to ensure that no one except *him* ever touched Ash again?

Draven slumped forward, resting his elbows on his knees and pressing the heels of his palms into his eye sockets, as though he could somehow physically shove his whirling thoughts back down into his subconscious where they belonged. His hands were shaking with a heady mixture of anger and fear. The sickening realization that he might have left things too late threatened to overwhelm him.

There and then, Draven made a decision. If Ash still lived, Draven would confess the depth of his feelings to the human the very next time they were alone together. He would stop hiding, and make sure Ash knew once and for all that Draven valued him more than he valued anything Ash might accomplish by selling himself.

He would tell Ash the truth.

No matter what.

SIX

"You must realize that I would happily see you dead, *veelaht*," Jontalyss Lusivian told Ash. The female Vithii's words were cold, though resentment burned beneath them like banked coals.

Ash was fairly certain he'd never seen anyone wield a bone-knitter *angrily* before—not even Ryder, the Shadow Wing's crusty and cynical medic. But the Adjunct's bondmate was doing so now, running the medical device's waveform emitter over the hairline crack in Ash's right ulna while simultaneously glaring at his offending forearm with enough vitriol to pierce the skin and melt the rest of his bones into slag.

"I don't doubt it," he replied in even tones, resisting the urge to twitch as the familiar deep itching of accelerated healing crawled through his flesh. "It must be terribly humiliating to have me here, right in your own home. Even more so, with Denrir's insistence on you patching his toy back together whenever he breaks it."

Jontalyss snarled something unintelligible at him and slammed the bone-knitter back into its storage unit inside the medikit. So far, the results of Ash's attempts to charm his way into some kind of accord with the beautiful Vithii woman had been... *iffy*. And that was being generous. Unsurprising, perhaps—since Ash's presence here basically embodied the Adjunct's contempt for his bondmate.

She was a politician's trophy wife, and had been since the day she'd accepted Denrir's mating bite. *Arm candy*, as humans said. That part was bad enough, but it was hardly an unusual practice in upper class Vithii circles. No, what really twisted Jontalyss Lusivian's knickers into a knot was the knowledge that her bondmate would rather screw a human male than screw her.

Of course, it wasn't news to anyone that Vithii sexual culture was a rolling clusterfuck of misogyny, power imbalance, and homophobia. Ash had learned far more than he'd ever wanted to about it over the past couple of years, mostly from the inside out. Now, he was stuck in arguably the most reviled role on the planet—surrogate boy-toy for a rich, repressed gay Vithii with anger management issues and a sense of entitlement the size of a planet.

Most Vithii swore blind that homosexuality didn't exist within their species. That was, of course, complete bullshit—but it played into the Vithii sense of superiority over the humans with whom they had shared the planet of Ilarius for the past hundred and twenty years or so.

The Vithii who were so inclined did what homosexuals always did within repressive cultures. They either quashed their inclinations completely for fear of the repercussions—which could be vicious—or they indulged in private trysts and tried not to get caught. But, as with pretty much everything else in life, the rules changed for those who reached a certain level of wealth and power.

As the Vithii's contempt and xenophobia toward humans had risen over the past couple of decades, it became acceptable in certain circles for powerful male Vithii to keep human body slaves. Which wasn't to say it was *legal*, precisely—but the law had become something of a gray area on Ilarius since the Regime came into power.

It was a polite fiction that human *seelahts* and *veelahts* weren't kept for sexual reasons, but rather for reasons of status. They were seen as advertisements for the natural order of things—dominant Vithii putting submissive humans in their place, as it should be the galaxy over. And if a male *veelaht* needed a Vithii owner's cock knotting his ass before he could truly understand who was in charge of things? Well, that was a reflection on the slave, not the owner. It wasn't as though the Vithii was fucking another male because he *wanted* to. He was just demonstrating his dominance over a stupid human slave—that was all.

And when he was so busy demonstrating that dominance over his male *veelaht* that he never seemed to have any time for his female Vithii bondmate? Well…

Jontalyss snatched up another medical device and waved it over Ash's arm, scowling at the readings.

"This says the break is healed," she snapped, not addressing his earlier words. Her frown deepened. "What's this swelling on the heel of your hand? The scanner is flagging it as a poison warning."

Ash huffed and pulled his arm away. "That's because you're using Vithii instrumentation. It's just a bee sting. One of the buzzing little menaces got into my room a few days ago, and it got me when I went to swat it."

Her nose wrinkled in distaste. "Filthy things. Someone should eradicate them."

Ash stretched carefully, trying not to wince at the array of aches and pains that seemed to make up his body these days.

"Perhaps not before scientists can come up with another species to pollinate the food crops," he said in a light tone. "But don't worry. Bee venom might be poison to Vithii, but it's merely a nuisance to humans unless they happen to be allergic... which I'm not."

Jontalyss made a noise of disgust, tossing her spikes of gold-highlighted hair. Her green eyes snapped fire. "Believe me. Worry for you is the last thing on my mind."

"I'm sure that's true." He shrugged on a loose shirt, moving stiffly as his shoulders and back protested. "Thank you for your help—even if it was given under duress. Anything involving the right arm is tricky to deal with when you're right-handed."

He'd assumed that the only response to his overture would be angry silence. That had been the pattern so far, at least, but she surprised him when he was almost to the door.

"Why did you come here, human?" The question sounded reluctant, like she wasn't quite sure she wanted to hear an answer that might make Ash more real—more of a person, less of an object. "You must have known what he's like. Why sign up to be his slave?"

Ash was exhausted, and he was also sporting additional injuries that he wasn't about to ask for her help in dealing with. But he stopped at the door and turned around to face her, leaning against the doorjamb. Denrir was gone for the day. It was quite likely that the Adjunct had the entire house bugged, but if he were careful, it would be safe enough for them to talk. And this was the first crack he'd seen so far in Jontalyss' armor—he wasn't about to let it slide.

"For money, of course," he lied.

She shook her head like she couldn't understand what he was saying. "But that's ridiculous. What good does money do you when you're stuck here? You must know that he's not just going to let you go when he gets tired of you. You've seen what he is. He'll kill you one day."

Ash let a wry smile stretch his lips. It felt like the expression no longer fit his face.

"I didn't say that the money was for *me*."

Her strong Vithii brows drew together in confusion, and he sighed.

"You must surely have some conception of what things are like out there these days, Jontalyss," he continued. "You're not *that* sheltered. I have a family. Parents who aren't getting any younger. I also had an older sister. I'd prefer not to see the same thing happen to them that happened to her."

Jontalyss was silent for a moment, as though debating with herself whether to continue.

"What happened to her?" she asked eventually.

Ash tried not to let anything show in his body language, even though this felt like a potential breakthrough with his recalcitrant target.

"Ten years ago, she was an outspoken critic of Minister Kovak, before he became Premiere. I feared for her safety, but our parents insisted the precautions they were taking for her security were sufficient." Ash paused, his eyes going far away. "They were wrong, and she later died in mysterious circumstances. Ever since then, I've been trying to find a way to get my mother and father to safety on Terra Nova. But I'm sure you're aware of how diffi-cult—and how *expensive*—that can be, for humans."

Some of those words were lies. But these days, lies were just about the only currency in which Ash traded.

Jontalyss' expression flickered at the mention of Terra Nova.

"The Premiere would not have to be so harsh, if humans like your sister did not defy the natural order of things," she said, but Ash could hear the trace of uncertainty in her voice.

"No doubt you're right," Ash said. "Though your bondmate would say that my presence here is part of the natural order of things. A human *veelaht* kneeling at the feet of his Vithii master—his *Fei'graal*. And yet, you appear to disagree on that subject."

Her expression closed off as the barb hit home. Ash took that as his cue to leave, so she could stew in those juices alone for a bit. As vital as cultivating this particular relationship might be, he still needed to rest and deal with the remainder of his injuries in private before the Adjunct returned in the evening, ready to mete out a fresh round of abuse. A tight band of instinctual panic tried to close around Ash's lungs at the thought, and he cursed the involuntary physical reaction to repeated trauma. He didn't have time for it. Not now, when he needed to sleep and heal.

Not *ever*, really.

The walls of the sprawling mansion felt like they were closing in around him as he trudged down to his quarters on the lowest level, not making eye contact with the stone-faced Vithii security guard who stood watch over the door at the top of the staircase.

One step at a time, he reminded himself firmly. *One minute at a time. Just keep moving forward toward the goal, and don't think about the rest.*

<hr>

Many cycles later, after Denrir had come and gone, Ash lay curled on the plasticrete floor of his spartan quarters. The first few days after he'd arrived at the Adjunct's property, his new *owner* had been tied up in Capital business that left him little time to indulge in his hobby of sadism. Ash had grown complacent; convincing himself that such extended absences would be the norm.

That was how things had been at the brothel, after all. There, he'd still had a fair amount of control over his schedule, with the ability to come and go as needed. He'd become reliant on a sort of pattern, where he'd get the crap beaten out of him, and then have a few days to recover before the next time.

He was also coming to realize how much he'd relied on regular contact with the handful of people he cared about on this shithole of a planet to keep him sane and focused. Draven. Ryder. Hunter and Kade. Pax and Nahleene. Skye and Temple.

Even though that contact had often come in the midst of one kind of crisis or another, it had still been part of his coping mechanism. And now, it was gone. He'd burned that bridge the moment he'd convinced Denrir to stage his death.

A selfish part of him had come to regret his decision over the past week, but an even *more* selfish part didn't. He'd planned the ruse for the sole purpose of ensuring that none of the brave fools he called friends tried to come after him if things went to hell… because it was a near certainty that things *would* go to hell. This way, if and when someone got killed, it would be Ash, and Ash alone.

There wasn't a damned thing any of the rest of them could do to convince Jontalyss Lusivian to contact her old university friend who was now the Terra Novan ambassador to Vithara—the original Vithii homeworld. There were, however, many things they could do to screw things up. Ensuring that the others thought he was dead, and therefore wouldn't come looking for him, had been a tactical decision—albeit a bloody difficult one to make.

But this way, he wouldn't have to worry about them crashing in with blasters blazing if he missed a check-in. If the stars aligned and Ash was successful, he would contact them as originally planned. True, on a personal level they would probably never forgive him for the ruse, but they were too dedicated and too professional a group not to follow through with the rest of the mission even when they were pissed off at him.

With luck, Pax and Nahleene were already on Maelfius, trying to garner support there for the humans on Ilarius. If Ash could deliver the Terra Novan ambassador into the mix, that would mean combined pressure on Vithara to rein in their upstart Ilarian Vithii cousins from two of the planet's largest trading partners. It would mean that the humans on Ilarius would no longer be fighting for their survival alone.

And given what the Adjunct had let slip tonight, outside help couldn't come soon enough. Somehow, on top of everything else, Ash needed to anonymously deliver his new little gem of intel somewhere it could do some good. The underground news outlets, perhaps.

Of course, before he could send an encrypted communiqué *or* deliver the Terra Novan ambassador, he needed to be able to stand up. Or crawl. Or… *something*. He turned his head, and his muscles shrieked in protest. The visual perspective of the room stretched like toffee, making the bed appear to be kilometers away from where he lay crumpled on the floor.

It was an illusion. He knew that. The damned bed was only a few steps away, and it would be much better for him if he could get into it. Better yet if he could get to the lav first and scrub a few layers of skin off in the shower, but Ash was a realist. That wasn't going to be happening anytime soon.

He tried to take stock.

Sex with Vithii males was tricky—and that was when they *weren't* also hell-bent on beating the shite out of you. Evolution was a strange thing, but it usually had a method to its madness. Vithii men had developed a band of tissue halfway along the length of their flexible cocks that swelled significantly after ejaculation, colloquially termed a *knot*. Vithii females, in turn, had strong muscles ringing the outer part of the vagina, which clamped down in response to penetration and orgasm, tying the mating pair together for a cycle or so until the knot went down.

It made sense from a reproductive standpoint. Vithii women entered a serenely trancelike state during knotting, pumping out happy, lovey-dovey bonding hormones while the knot ensured that the male's sperm had the best possible chance of reaching a fertile egg rather than leaking out and being wasted. Males, meanwhile, tended toward an unfiltered brain-to-mouth stream of consciousness during knotting, as the hormonal surge lowered their inhibitions.

That last bit had led to some interesting tidbits of intelligence slipping past Denrir's guard on a handful of occasions, to be sure. And while the intel gained from those slips had never been Ash's primary objective in this venture, it was a useful secondary benefit.

Of course, much of the Vithii's clever evolutionary adaptation was moot when the receiving partner was human. Not to mention male. When it came to being the *veelaht* of a Vithii sadist, all it meant was that you were stuck taking whatever punishment the bastard wanted to dish out while simultaneously being in the most vulnerable position imaginable, with a hard knot of swollen tissue jammed mercilessly against your prostate the whole time. And prophets help you if you struggled.

All of which circled neatly back to the present situation.

If Ash ignored the anal tearing—which he was most definitely trying to do right now—then it was his ribs that were the biggest problem. He was willing to bet that at least two were broken. Rather oddly, that would be a first for him. He'd never had broken ribs before. The brothel had maintained a minimal number of house rules surrounding use of their *seelahts* and *veelahts* for hire—one of which was '*no broken bones.*' Just Ash's luck that he'd apparently landed a *Fei'graal* with a kink for exactly that.

Gods above. He needed to do something besides just lie here like a discarded dishrag. Panic prickled the edges of his awareness at the realization that there was nothing to stop Denrir from coming back in a few cycles. Nothing to stop him delivering a fresh round of torment before he left for his job in the government complex in the morning. And Ash... wasn't entirely sure what he'd do, if that happened while he was in his present state.

The door to his quarters slid open, throwing his heart into a mad staccato rhythm at the idea that Denrir might have returned already. A red haze haloed the edges his vision.

He couldn't break yet. It was too soon... he hadn't accomplished what he'd come here to do. Not even close.

Soft footsteps entered.

"You know you're not the first *veelaht* he's had, right?" said a female voice. "I think you're, like, the seventh? Four of them ended up dying within the first month after he brought them here. He was going on and on last night about how he thought you'd last longer than most. Though I have to say, human... I'm not really seeing it right now."

SEVEN

"Sorry to disappoint," Ash rasped, his pulse slowly returning to normal. "And, by the way, if you brought the medikit along, you will officially have become my favorite person on the planet."

Legs and feet encased in a tailored pantsuit and practical pumps stepped into his hazy field of vision. A moment later, the kit thumped to the floor in front of him. Ash wet his lips and swallowed, hating how the swelling where Denrir's fingers had dug into the tender flesh of his throat made the collar feel even tighter than it had been to start with.

"Brilliant. I don't suppose I could trouble you for a pair of trousers while you're at it?" he asked.

Jontalyss raked her bitter gaze over his nakedness and raised an eyebrow. "Why? Clothes won't make you any less of a walking hole for his cock. Besides, you don't look like you'd be able to get them on by yourself, anyway."

Ash sighed, and regretted it instantly as his ribs screamed a protest. "Yes. Well… fair points. Can't really dispute either one of them."

The promise of relief lent him the strength to roll carefully into a sitting position, gritting his teeth against the pain. Jontalyss had wandered across the room and was now perched daintily on the edge of the bed—proving Ash's earlier hypothesis that the damned thing hadn't been that far away after all. He opened the medikit with shaking fingers, taking the bone-knitter out and starting work on his battered ribcage.

Ryder would be either angry as hell or utterly appalled if she knew how much competence he'd gained in this one very specific little corner of emergency medicine. More likely, both at once. It was just as well that she'd never have cause to find out. He clenched his teeth harder against the unexpected ache of loneliness caused by that thought.

"You're really a rather pathetic creature, aren't you," Jontalyss observed.

"Very," Ash agreed, not being in any real position to argue with her at the moment.

A pause. "It's hard to believe such a weak thing as you seem to be would do something like this to help other people."

"Is it?" he asked absently, as the stabbing pain in his chest began to ease under the infrared healing waves.

"Yes."

The silence stretched while he held himself stiffly, keeping the damaged area as still as possible while the bone-knitter did its work. When breathing in no longer felt like the grinding of broken glass against his left lung, he breached the quiet of the room.

"So, what about you, Frey Lusivian?" he asked, using the female honorific with only a hint of irony. "You've already heard my story, but how did you end up bonded to such a rich and powerful monster?"

More silence. Ash was beginning to think that his current battered state had played hell with his ability to read a mark's mood, when she finally spoke.

"I got greedy," Jontalyss said in a monotone.

Ash nodded, and covered a wince when his neck protested. "Mmm. Happens to the best of us, I suppose. How did the two of you meet?"

Jontalyss shifted on the edge of the mattress. "Through my parents. My mother is an administrative assistant in the office where Denrir works. My father had been a generous party donor before his business failed during the last downturn. They got me an invitation to a Regime reception where they knew several eligible party officials would be mingling."

"And you caught Denrir's eye?" Ash said, starting work on the swelling where the Adjunct had strangled him, repeatedly cutting off his air in an attempt to panic him into fighting the knot in his arse. The trick with these kinds of injuries was to heal as much of the underlying tissue damage as possible without eradicating the visible bruises. Arseholes like Denrir did *so* enjoy leaving their mark behind.

Jontalyss shrugged one shoulder, not looking at him directly.

"I'm not surprised that you did," Ash told her. "You're quite a lovely woman."

At that, she snorted. "As if he cares anything for lovely *women*."

"Appearances are important in Denrir's world," Ash said. "As I'm certain you're painfully aware."

Her expression went hard and distant. "Yeah," she murmured. "You could say that."

Okay. Wrong tack.

Ash stretched his neck cautiously from side to side, feeling out the range of motion. "Well, since we're both stuck here with him for now, why don't you tell me more about yourself." He set the deep-tissue regenerator aside and shook out a single-dose universal antibiotic pill, swallowing it dry. "You're young. Did you go to university?"

As subtlety went, it wasn't up to his usual standards. At the moment, though, it was about all he had to offer. Keep her talking. Lay the groundwork and hope he lived long enough to build on it.

Jontalyss' eyes softened and grew distant. "I'm not *that* young. But yes. I did. On Vithara."

"Oh? That's interesting. What did you study on Vithara?"

"Environmental Law with a minor in Communications."

Ash whistled low. "Sounds like you had ambitions of your own," he said, as he measured out a double-dose of analgesic and another of electrolytes.

The light that had briefly kindled in her green eyes dimmed. "Once, maybe."

He set everything back in the kit and gave her his full attention. "The present doesn't necessarily inform the future." *Please, gods and prophets—let the present not inform the future.* "Just because you've set those ambitions aside for now, doesn't mean they're lost forever."

She eyed him, trying for haughty and falling a bit short of the mark. "Says the naked human patching himself up with a borrowed medikit after being beaten and knotted by his owner."

Ash mimed a shot to the heart. "*Touché.* Though I'd like to think that our situations aren't *quite* the same."

Bitterness washed over her sculpted features. "No. You're right. You get fucked. I get vials of his stored saliva to inject into my mating gland every few days, so Denrir can present the fiction in public that he's maintaining our bond."

Ash filed that bit of information away. It answered the question of whether Denrir was willing or able to play the part of heterosexual bondmate in any kind of meaningful capacity. Clearly, he wasn't. And Jontalyss' obvious bitterness over that fact might help Ash get her on his side, given enough time.

In a healthy Vithii bonding, the male spouse initiated regular sexual contact that involved licking and biting the female's mating gland, located at the base of her neck. Without that contact, the female's endocrine system began to shut down production of mating markers within a few weeks. This change was clearly distinguishable by scent, at least for other Vithii.

For a female Vithii, being *grei'kaapt*—widowed or abandoned by her mate—was an extreme social stigma rather than a simple biological process. For that reason, there were a host of medical treatments available to mask the effects of mating withdrawal, though they tended to be insanely expensive and to lose effectiveness over time. Denrir clearly preferred the cheaper route of spitting into a container and sticking it in the freezer for his spurned mate to use as needed.

Ash wasn't too shocked by that, to be honest. It demonstrated an added layer of contempt and emotional cruelty of the type that seemed to be right down the Adjunct's alley.

"If it helps," he said mildly, "I've had Vithii men before, and Denrir's cock ranks *way* down in the bottom quartile somewhere. Believe me when I say—you're not missing much."

That startled a harsh bark of laughter from Jontalyss, before she recovered herself and glared at him. "That's not funny," she said, despite clear evidence to the contrary.

It was Ash's turn to shrug, as he packed away the contents of the medikit and snapped it closed.

"Schoolyard insults are about all I'm up for at the moment, I'm afraid," he said, as he tested his balance and clambered carefully to his feet, bringing the kit with him and gesturing at it. "Thank you for this, by the way."

She tossed her head, conveying disdain that didn't *quite* ring true after the last few minutes. "Denrir squanders his wealth buying a new *veelaht* whenever he breaks the old one. As long as he continues to support this sham of a bonding, half of that money is mine. I'm just trying to be frugal."

Ash let a soft snort escape. "An eminently practical outlook, Frey Lusivian. But thank you, nonetheless."

Jontalyss snatched the kit from his grasp as though she feared catching some kind of disease if she touched him directly. She didn't actually say "*Hmph!*" as she flounced out of the room, but Ash still took the sentiment as read.

When she was gone, the heavy door sliding shut behind her, he let out a slow sigh and limped over to the bed. The dermal regenerator he'd liberated on his second night in the house lay hidden under the mattress where he'd left it last time. Now that he no longer had an audience, he'd deal with the less savory aspects of medical care and try to spend the remainder of the night sleeping, instead of obsessing over what fresh torture the morning might bring.

———◆———

The following days continued a pattern that Ash knew he could only maintain for so long. Denrir's responsibilities in the Capital did not keep him from home very often, and Ash bore the brunt of that lull in the Adjunct's government workload. On all but a couple occasions, Jontalyss showed up a cycle or two later with the medikit and a wall of stony bitterness that he was finding it slow work to breach.

Seen through human eyes, the culture of *seelahts* and *veelahts* was an odd thing. One might expect that Ash and those like him would be physical prisoners as well as societal ones, but that was not… precisely the case. Yes, the door on Ash's spartan quarters *could* be locked from the outside, making it into a cell. But it generally wasn't, and wouldn't be unless he was foolish enough to be caught doing something he shouldn't.

The point of possessing a human body slave was to demonstrate one's inherent Vithii dominance and superiority. The thrill came from the knowledge that you owned and controlled another sentient being so thoroughly that they were subject to your will, submitting to you without obvious coercion.

In reality, most unfortunate humans who ended up in such a situation were simply too frightened of what punishments they might receive if they stepped out of line to rebel. And, more to the point, despite the horror stories of grisly murder and abuse that regularly made the rounds, most Vithii owners were far less twisted and sadistic than Denrir. For many body slaves, the choice was between starving on the streets in the Capital… or having food and a roof over one's head in exchange for sex on demand, regular humiliation, and perhaps the occasional bruise here or there.

The practical upshot was that Ash had the freedom to come and go within the Adjunct's sprawling mansion of a house provided he didn't do anything that would anger his owner, like snooping in private areas or walking in on guests. Of course, that might have been very different, had Denrir known the extent of Ash's skills with tech. But one thing about being a human hiding in plain sight around Vithii bigots—you didn't have to work at being underestimated. It was the default reaction.

And that was how Ash was able to get a message out to the most reliable of the underground media outlets, using a personal comm unit that a member of Denrir's private security contingent left sitting unattended in one of the common rooms. In the message, Ash outlined what he'd learned from the Adjunct during an—*ahem*—unguarded moment, when Denrir had taunted Ash about the Premiere's proposed plan to construct fenced internment camps for humans in the Capital who were found to be 'undesirable elements' in society.

Anyone who'd studied either human or Vitharan history could decipher *that* unwritten code in about two seconds flat, and it only helped to reinforce Ash's suspicion that things were approaching the endgame of this tragic political farce. True, he might have felt better if he'd been able to get this particular piece of intel directly into his friends' hands, but it simply wasn't practical right now.

They'd hear about it soon enough, once the secure message boards started blowing up with the news.

He trusted Hunter and Kade to see to it that the Shadow Wing's human members were kept as safe as possible… present company excepted, obviously.

Because—as alarming as the news about human internment camps might be—that wasn't Ash's primary objective. No, his primary objective was still walking around with abandonment issues and a giant chip on her shoulder. It was Ash's job to somehow turn Jontalyss' personal bitterness against their mutual tormenter into an alliance.

Preferably, an alliance that led to Jontalyss contacting her old bestie from university, Isidora Martinez—the human ambassador to Vithara, and their best hope for offworld support to stop a lunatic's plans for genocide.

EIGHT

It took Draven a lot longer than he would have liked to find out the location of Denrir Lusivian's private retreat outside of the Capital. He'd left a message with Jonah shortly after he liberated the records of Ash's sale to the Adjunct, so Jonah could update the others regarding what he'd found.

Now, he was speaking with Jonah again, this time with a request to pass on rather than a briefing. Draven was well aware of how brazen of him it was to ask Hunter and the others for *anything* after the way he'd left the lunar station. And this was… not a small request. He was taking it on faith that his comrades wouldn't simply throw him to the *greilo*-beasts instead of acting on his vague and questionable plans and theories.

"Have they contacted you since the last message I sent?" he asked Jonah.

"Have they *contacted* me?" Jonah echoed, his voice rising in incredulity. "Dude, they've been practically yelling my ear off for the last few days! I'm supposed to tell you not to even *think* about going to that guy's place on your own, and to contact them directly before you do *anything*."

"Give me a break. Why do you think I'm using you as a go-between?" Draven muttered. "It's so I don't have to listen to that noise."

"Yeah, that must be nice for you," Jonah groused. "Anyway, I told you what they said, like I was supposed to. Now, what do you need?"

Draven took a deep breath and rattled off a series of coordinates, a time code, and what he needed to have waiting at that time and location.

Silence crackled for a beat.

"You serious?" Jonah asked uncertainly.

Draven swallowed a growl. "Just pass it on for me, kid. They'll either make it happen somehow, or they'll tell me to go fuck myself. I'm still going in, either way. Make sure to let them know I'll be trying to retrieve the original target as well. That might help."

"I'll let them know," Jonah said, still sounding unsure. "Just… be careful, man. All right?"

"I'm always careful," Draven told him, and cut off the transmission before Jonah could respond. He looked around the dingy substation, and sighed. Everything he needed was in place, or soon would be. He'd have to give the others time to get his escape route set up—assuming they were going to—but once that was done, it was way past time to go and find the answers he needed.

Two days later, Draven snuck onto the Adjunct's estate. It was the middle of the night, and he'd left the ancient hovercar he'd purchased with some of Kade's cash hidden in a wooded area about half a klick away from the property boundary. It was a calculated risk not having it closer, but he had no way of knowing if Lusivian had satellite or drone surveillance over the area.

It would be a lot easier for a single Vithii to sneak up in the dark on foot than in a four-seater vehicle with a great big shiny heat signature. Especially a vehicle with exhaust port issues as loud as the ones on the heap of scrap he'd managed to acquire from someone in the undercity who would ask no questions. During his preparations, he'd also acquired night vision goggles and a recent real estate parcel map of the area. This part of the Capital's outskirts was the purview of the very rich—people who worked in the city but could afford to get away from its crime, congestion, and pollution once the workday was done.

Everything out here sat on its own generous hectarage, isolated from its neighbors by distance and carefully cultivated woodland. That at least meant Draven wouldn't be dealing with nosy neighbors calling the security forces on him for skulking around the place at such an odd time of night. Still, this kind of money looked out for itself, and there would be plenty of private security to deal with, he was sure.

He had a pack with everything he could think of that might come in handy, but unfortunately this particular brand of breaking and entering had never been his specialty. He could bluff his way into a place with the best of them, but the whole *sneaking* thing wasn't really his forte.

That was why he also had a small arsenal of weapons stashed in the pack, in addition to the blaster strapped to his thigh and the daggers sheathed in his boots.

Draven managed to find and disable the generator powering the electrified fence around the property without too much trouble. He also managed to cut through the heavy chainlink without making noise enough to wake the dead, and squeezed inside the resulting gap.

He was skirting the perimeter of the ridiculously ostentatious mansion set in the middle of the property—looking for a delivery entrance that might lead into the lower levels—when a motion sensor light flared into life. The sudden light source made his night-vision goggles bloom into a blank vista of solid green. Draven reached up to rip them off, but a stun beam caught him in the shoulder before he could complete the gesture.

He crashed to the ground an instant later, helpless.

The stun effect wore off quickly since it had only been a glancing strike. Unfortunately, it didn't wear off until a pair of private security guards had already descended on Draven, stripping him of his weapons and equipment before zip-tying his wrists behind his back. Draven lay facedown in the grass, silently cursing himself for being ten kinds of fool.

"Is he awake?" one of the goons asked. "Good. Comm the Adjunct and ask what he wants us to do with the intruder."

The other goon moved a few steps away and spoke into a communication device. Draven tried to look around—to see if he could maybe take down the closest guard with a leg sweep or something—but he came face to face with a blaster muzzle instead.

"Don't move," the first goon said simply.

Draven clenched his jaw, and kept still. With luck, they'd take him inside. That was where he'd been trying to get anyway, so once he was there, he'd just have to think of something.

"Well?" the goon with the blaster prompted. "What did he say?"

"His comm's turned off," replied the second goon. "I woke his bondmate instead. She said take the prisoner down to the *veelaht*'s cell in the basement, and we'd find him there."

Draven's heart stuttered, and it wasn't because of the stun blast.

The first goon made a noise of disgust. "Great. Like I really need to see that shit firsthand tonight."

"Stop bitching," said the second. "I just get paid to do what the fuck I'm told, not to have an opinion about it."

The first goon grumbled something that sounded uncomplimentary, and then the pair were dragging Draven to his feet. His stomach lurched as the aftereffects of the stun beam made his insides try to take a trip to visit his outsides, but he swallowed back the bile and kept everything where it was supposed to be. The blaster muzzle jabbed him in the side.

"Move your feet and keep your mouth shut," said the disgruntled goon. "The sooner I can get this over with, the better."

Draven kept his mouth shut and let himself be frog-marched inside, through the very entrance he'd been hoping to sneak in through. As he'd assumed, it led to a drab basement level. He had a vague impression of storage areas and HVAC systems, but then they were approaching an open area with a door leading off one side. The door looked sturdy, and it had a locking pad next to it. It was also open.

"Sir?" called the second goon, while they were still some distance away.

There was a beat of silence before an irritated voice emerged from within the cell-like room. "What are you doing down here at this time of night? I'm busy—go away!"

The goons exchanged a look around Draven, still restrained between them. For his part, Draven felt alternating waves of hot and cold prickle across his body as his stun-scrambled brain realized who else must be inside that room.

"Apologies, sir," said the other goon. "We've captured a heavily armed intruder attempting to break into the house. Your bondmate told us to bring him down here to you."

Another pause.

Then a middle-aged Vithii with a pugnacious jaw and iron gray hair emerged from the room. He was, Draven saw with relief, fully clothed. Even so, rage threatened to cut off his vision in a haze of coppery red as Denrir *fucking* Lusivian sauntered over to them—looking down his nose at Draven as though Draven were nothing more than dirt on his polished designer shoe.

"I'll need to have a word with my dearest bondmate about discretion, it seems," Lusivian muttered, as if to himself. Then he sighed. "Very well. I suppose we'd better hold onto him for the moment. We should find out if he's important or not before we kill him."

Yeah? Someone's fucking well going to die before long, Draven thought, glaring daggers at the slimy bastard. *But I fully intend it to be you, not me.*

Lusivian either didn't register the death-glare, or he didn't care.

"You can lock him in the *veelaht*'s cell for now," he said carelessly, before turning back to the open doorway and snapping, "Cur! Come here!" in a voice of command.

Despite his swimming head, Draven held his breath, bracing himself not to react as a lithe human figure emerged from the doorway, head bowed to shield his face behind a curtain of loose, black hair. He was completely naked except for the leather collar buckled around his neck. The dusky olive canvas of his skin was covered in bruises.

Draven's gaze fell on a set of dark imprints spanning the human's hips—the clear shapes of grasping fingers. He barely managed to clamp down on the roar of rage that wanted to claw its way free of his throat, but he was sure that it had to be screaming from his eyes instead.

Ash sank gracefully into a kneeling position at the Adjunct's feet, sneaking the barest glance at Draven as he did. Draven thought he saw an instant of blank shock in those dark eyes before the human dipped his head again.

He tried to take stock. Ash was weaponless and unprotected, and all three Vithii were large, healthy males. But Draven knew better than to discount Ash, even now. True, Draven was restrained and covered by a weapon, but this might still be their best chance to get free. The odds weren't great, but they weren't the worst Draven had ever faced, either. He tried to catch Ash's eye again, hoping to somehow convey that they should take advantage of the element of surprise, but the human did not look up at him.

"It appears I'll have need of your cage for a few cycles, cur," Lusivian said with a cruel smile. "You may have the honor of accompanying me upstairs to my room for the rest of the night."

"Yes, *Fei'graal*," Ash said in a low, compliant tone that was completely unlike his normal way of speaking.

Draven tried to will the human to look up, but it was Lusivian's attention that fell on him instead. The Adjunct's eyes narrowed.

"Now, what brings you to my door, I wonder?" Lusivian asked. "Burglary? But no… if you were *heavily armed*, that tells a different story entirely."

Draven drew breath to say something unwise, but a soft voice cut in.

"He is here for me, *Fei'graal*," Ash said, still not looking up. "This is the man I told you about."

A sense of wrongness jolted through Draven with roughly the same impact as the stun beam that had hit him earlier. He blinked, certain that he must have misheard—

Lusivian's eyebrows went up. "The man you…?" he began, only to cut himself off. "Oh, you mean the criminal? Good prophets—and he actually thought you were important enough to come here after you in such a ridiculous fashion?"

"It was what I feared would happen, *Fei'graal*—yes," Ash murmured, hunching his shoulders further inward… the picture of humility and self-effacement. Draven felt his world tipping on its axis. Bile rose in his throat again.

Lusivian laughed, long and deep. "Gods above. And here I thought I was merely indulging a pet when you first fed me that preposterous story."

"As I told you then, this man is obsessed with me, *Fei'graal*," Ash said, sounding miserable. "He knew he could never afford my purchase price, but I was certain he would try to come after me anyway. I'd hoped that by making it appear I'd been killed, I could prevent anything like this from happening."

Lusivian's expression shifted, a certain territorialism creeping into it as he looked at Draven more closely. Draven couldn't help the snarl that curled his upper lip in return, even as metaphorical bedrock shifted beneath him, wracked by the tremors of Ash's apparent betrayal.

The Adjunct breathed out sharply through his nose, a contemptuous sound. "Well," he said, "I suppose this *does* change things. You said this man was wanted by the Regime, cur?"

"Indeed, *Fei'graal*," Ash replied without hesitation. "He is part of a subversive group responsible for sabotage and rebel incitement. He bragged to me repeatedly about the size of the reward for his capture. I gather the security forces could gain quite a bit of important information from his interrogation."

Draven fought vertigo as the horrible, swirling sense of *impossibility* swamped him yet again.

"*Ash*," he whispered, the word slipping past his control and disappearing into the chasm that suddenly seemed to loom between them.

"Do not presume to speak to my property, *criminal*," Lusivian barked. "Guards, lock him up. Stay here and watch the cell. I will contact someone from the security forces to come for him in the morning."

The goons manhandled Draven toward the open door of the cell.

"Come along, cur," Lusivian said crisply, and Draven twisted around, getting a brief glimpse of Ash rising smoothly to his feet and following the Adjunct.

Then he was shoved forward through the entrance, staggering as he tried to compensate for his bound hands. The door rolled shut behind him with an air of finality.

Draven stumbled and landed on his knees, breathing hard. Again, his stomach tried to rebel, and again, he forced it back down. For long moments, he knelt there in a sort of daze, replaying the last few minutes in hopes that it would somehow change what had happened.

It didn't help.

What he'd just heard Ash say could not be reconciled with what he'd always known to be true about the human. Ash would never betray him in such a way… yet Ash *had* just betrayed him in such a way. Both things could not be reality.

Eventually, he realized that he was still sitting there on the plasticrete floor, staring at nothing. By force of will, he dragged his eyes into focus and made himself take in his surroundings. The room was a square box, with a bed whose purpose he refused to think about, a dresser with the legs bolted to the floor, a latrine set in the corner, and not much else.

Draven knew he needed to act, whether Ash was a traitor or not. Even so, it took several more minutes before he could focus enough to think beyond the continuous mantra of denial looping inside his brain. Finally, though, practicality reared its head.

If they'd used regular handcuffs on him, he could've gotten his hands around in front of him by hitching his hips and legs through the space between his bound arms, even though it would've meant pulled shoulder muscles for someone with his build. But the zip tie didn't leave enough room for that.

Fortunately, the idiot guards had left him his boots, even if they'd found and removed the daggers hidden inside them. He shuffled around on his bruised knees until he was sitting on his heels, and fumbled for the laces on the right boot. Untying them blind like this was a total pain in the ass, but he eventually managed to do so. Threading the loose end through the tight loop of the zip tie and getting hold of it again was an even worse pain in the ass. Once he'd done it, tying that loose end to the still-tied laces on his other boot wasn't too bad.

Draven awkwardly rolled onto his side, and pedaled his legs in a rapid motion like someone riding a stupidly small bicycle. The length of braided polysynth bootlace sawed back and forth against the plastic zip tie. The binding dug into his wrists painfully, but Draven could feel the heat of friction growing where the two materials rubbed together. It barely took a minute before the zip tie snapped, the pressure on his wrists falling away.

He rolled into a sitting position and shook the kinks out, then quickly retied his bootlaces. With a deep breath, he shoved everything else away, and looked around for anything that might be useful as a weapon whenever the guards came back and unlocked the door.

NINE

Ash followed the Adjunct meekly, trying not to let the mad staccato rhythm of his pulse bleed through into his body language. Static fizzed around the edges of his awareness as his brain fought his instincts for control.

He'd already been sinking into that distant, disconnected place where his consciousness hid when the pain started. It was a place deep inside himself where he could still submit to simple demands, but where nothing that was being done to his body could truly touch him. In the times between rounds of torture, Ash was self-aware enough to know that he was gradually ceding ground—his mission to subvert Jontalyss to the Shadow Wing's side morphing by degrees into a mission of mere survival.

He'd been losing the game, and in doing so, he was also losing *himself*.

When he'd glanced up and seen Draven held between two of the private security guards, he'd thought for a moment that it was a hallucination, or maybe a dream. Draven's presence here didn't mesh with his current reality. Dragging his mind back into full awareness and engaging his wits while kneeling naked and collared at the Adjunct's feet had been one of the more difficult things Ash had ever done in his life.

Imagining what Draven's face must have looked like when Ash calmly threw him under the hoverbus would likely send him plunging right back into the mental abyss. For that reason, he didn't try.

He needed to think.

He *couldn't* think.

So he walked with his head bowed, two steps behind the Vithii he called *Fei'graal*. Master. The base of his palm itched and burned, as though the tiny ampoule of bee venom hidden beneath his skin was trying to claw its way out. In the space of five minutes, everything had just come crashing down around him. The only options remaining to him were all catastrophically bad ones.

But he still needed to take action. Draven was locked in a cell in the basement beneath him, and if he fell into the Regime's hands…

Ahead of him, Denrir stopped in front of the door belonging to one of the off-duty private guards and pounded on it. Fresh panic trickled through Ash's veins. He might be able to do what he needed to do if he was alone with the Adjunct, but if Denrir intended to keep a guard with him tonight, Ash's odds of survival—much less success— dropped to almost nothing.

The guard opened the door, bleary-eyed and dressed in sleep clothes. His gaze flickered over Ash's nakedness and an expression of distaste— quickly masked—passed over his coarse features.

"What's wrong, sir?" he asked his employer. "Is there an emergency?"

"Yes, but you already slept through it," Denrir said with a sneer. "Contact the Security Intendant's office and leave a message that I've captured a wanted fugitive with a price on his head. Tell him to contact me first thing in the morning to arrange for prisoner transport."

"Yes, sir," said the guard. "Is there anything else?"

"When you've done that, wake the others and have them secure the perimeter of the property. It seems this intruder was most likely working alone, but I intend to take no chances."

"I'll see to it," said the rumpled guard.

Denrir nodded sharply and turned on his heel, heading toward the upper level. Ash followed, trying not to worry about whether Draven had dragged any of their other friends here with him.

It didn't matter. His next step was clear, either way. He cursed himself for not managing to stop the Adjunct from getting a message out about the break-in. Still, having the four off-duty guards posted outside the house rather than inside might be helpful, at least to start with. And thankfully, his thoughts were beginning to clear under the rush of fresh adrenaline pumping through his veins.

He followed Denrir into his private bedroom, every nerve stretched taut. There were too many things that could go wrong in the next handful of minutes. Far, far too many.

"Kneel," Denrir ordered. "Obviously, you will be punished for allowing filth like that to touch you when you were a common whore. I indulged you when you spun me your tale of woe and asked for my help in faking your death, but now I have been inconvenienced by your philandering on not merely one occasion, but two."

Ash sank to his knees, guessing what would come next. Behind him, Denrir's footsteps receded, and Ash heard the sound of a closet door sliding open. Denrir didn't keep his collection of whips, restraints, and other torture devices in the basement. No, he kept them lovingly stored and maintained here, in his room, and brought down with him only what he desired to use each time he tormented Ash.

While the man was distracted with picking the perfect implement of punishment, Ash lifted his left hand and silently tore into the fleshy base of his thumb with his teeth, ignoring the way the pain made his eyes sting. The tiny packet implanted under his skin was made of EM-reflective material that blocked most scanners. He snagged the edge with his teeth and pulled it out. Then he grabbed the corner of the scan resistant packaging and tore it open.

The micro-injector hidden inside fell into his bloody palm. The little tube-shaped device was barely a centimeter long, and less than half that in width. He grasped it between the thumb and forefinger of his uninjured hand—desperate not to fumble it—and felt around for the button recessed in the thing's base. Ash depressed it with the edge of a ragged fingernail, and a tiny, spring-loaded needle popped out of the other end.

The closet door slid shut and Denrir returned, still out of Ash's line of sight. The sound of a whip slapping lightly against a clothed thigh cut across the uneven noise of Ash's breathing. His neck prickled as his tormenter stepped up behind him.

"I will enjoy the next few minutes immensely, cur," The Adjunct nearly purred.

"Somehow I doubt that," Ash told him, and surged to his feet.

He whirled as he rose, jabbing the point of the tiny needle into the side of Denrir's neck and squeezing the micro-injector's base between his thumb and forefinger to force its contents beneath the Vithii's skin. Denrir flailed, a meaty fist catching Ash in the side of the face and sending him staggering.

It was too late, though. The injector had done its job. All Ash had to do now was keep the Adjunct from getting out of this room and seeking help in the next few minutes.

The Vithii slapped a palm against his neck as if in surprise. "Wh-what did you do?"

Ash stared at the Adjunct's flushed face and wide eyes, and tried—without success—to feel something. *Anything*.

"I killed you," he said simply, tossing the spent injector onto the end of the bed, where he wouldn't lose track of it during the next few minutes. "I'd apologize, but we both know I wouldn't mean it."

Denrir let out a choked roar and charged him. Ash ducked to the side, hoping that anyone close enough to hear the racket would assume it was just the Adjunct railing at him as he beat him. The Vithii staggered like an enraged bull, swiping a fist toward Ash's head again.

Already, Denrir's breath was coming in wheezing gasps as the area around the injection site swelled up like a balloon. Vithii had been latecomers to the colony on Ilarius, which had already been settled by humans for decades by the time their refugee ships had arrived. Humans… who brought along with them all of the necessary components for planting, pollinating, and harvesting their food crops.

It was merely happenstance that the honeybees they'd introduced into the Ilarian ecosystem produced a defensive venom that killed Vithii in minutes if they were stung too close to an airway. The tiny implantable device Ash had smuggled into the Adjunct's house beneath his skin had cost a small fortune on the black market. It had also leaked, making Ash's palm itch like blazes, and set off a warning on the medical scanner Jontalyss had used on him when his arm was broken not long after he first arrived.

But not all of the venom had leaked out. And it was doing the job it had been designed for, nevertheless.

Denrir crashed around the room, trying to take out his rage on Ash, rather than doing the intelligent thing and running for the nearest person who could call emergency services. Ash ducked and dodged until he got an opening to slam his body into the Vithii's back, sending them both crashing to the ground with Ash on top.

The Adjunct roared again, but there was a definite gurgle behind it this time. Ash got the flailing arm that wasn't scrabbling at his rapidly swelling neck twisted into a hammerlock. He grabbed Denrir's hair with his other hand, using the grip to mash his victim's face into the carpot.

It wasn't ideal—Ash was still bleeding DNA evidence all over the soon-to-be corpse and the rug beneath it. But this was no longer a stealth operation. Draven's arrival had seen to that.

Denrir bucked beneath him as his body fought the effects of suffocation, the sounds he was making growing ever more garbled until the swelling cut off his airway completely. When he finally went limp—his heart stuttering out its last few beats before going silent—Ash rose on shaky legs and stared down at the motionless body, blinking.

He retrieved the micro-injector and went into the en-suite bathroom, where he flushed the thing down the commode. Then he cleaned up his hand, closing the wound with a dermal regenerator he found in the top drawer of the sink cabinet. With unsteady fingers, he unbuckled the collar around his neck and threw it aside with a violent movement before returning to the bedroom. There, he rummaged around until he found a too-large shirt and a pair of exercise shorts with a drawstring waist that he could use to cover himself.

As Ash had suspected, Denrir kept a personal sidearm stashed in one of his desk drawers. It was a small laser pistol with no stun setting. Ash took it and crossed the room, palming open the closet door. He stared dispassionately at the collection of implements of sexual torture hanging on neat rows of hooks. Then he reached for a pair of metal handcuffs and the key that went with them, before turning and leaving the room.

Jontalyss' bedroom was at the far end of the wing. Hopefully, that would mean she'd slept through her bondmate's murder, assuming she went back to sleep after the commotion of Draven's capture.

She hadn't.

When he opened the door, it was to find her huddled on the bed with the lights on low and another small laser pistol pointed at him. The barrel was shaking visibly.

When she spoke, her voice was shaking just as badly as her aim. "Don't come any closer! Tell me what's going on!"

Ash sighed, and strode toward her with his own sidearm aimed unwaveringly at her shoulder, where it hopefully wouldn't kill her if he had to use it. She would either squeeze the trigger on him, or she wouldn't… and with the way the pistol was wavering, he'd give it fifty-fifty odds that the beam would even hit him if she did.

When he was close enough, he grabbed the trembling pistol out of her hand and tossed it away. She curled in on herself, staring up at him with wide eyes.

"Are you going to kill me?" she asked in a tiny voice.

"Not hardly," he said. "I've put too much bloody work into you—though I expect that's all gone down the drain now."

Pulling the handcuffs free from where he'd hooked them over his waistband, he snapped a bracelet around her nearest wrist one-handed, and snapped the other around a slat of the wrought iron headboard that even Vithii strength wouldn't be able to break. After a quick sweep to make sure there was nothing within arm's reach that she might somehow be able to use to free herself, he turned his attention back to her.

"No one's going to hurt you," he said. "I'll be back soon, assuming the guards don't manage to kill me first. If they do, then they'll find you soon enough."

He tossed the handcuff key onto the dresser across the room and headed out, ignoring her frantic cry of "*Wait!*" as the door slid shut behind him.

Bare feet did have one advantage—the guards never heard him coming as he returned to the lower level. The two Denrir had left on watch were guarding the locked door of his *veelaht*'s quarters, just as they'd been ordered. His blood racing with adrenaline, Ash shot the first one through the heart, and shot the second one in the side as he scrambled for a weapon. He collapsed, groaning and clutching at the hole in his gut, only to go silent when Ash finished him off with a single head shot at close range.

Doing his best to ignore his racing heartbeat and the beads of clammy sweat popping out across his face, Ash dragged the nearest guard's hand up to press against the palm sensor of the lock. The door slid open and Draven barreled out, holding an empty dresser drawer in both hands like a club. He skidded to a halt upon seeing the path of destruction Ash had cut to get to him, and the makeshift weapon clattered to the floor.

For a long moment, they stared at each other in tense silence, both of them breathing hard.

TEN

Draven broke first. "You fucking *bastard*! I thought you'd turned on us. What the fuck were you thinking, disappearing like that? The others thought you were *dead*!"

His volume increased with every word, and then he was in Ash's face, crowding him backward until Ash's bruised shoulders thumped against the wall behind him. Through a gathering haze of reaction he couldn't afford to give in to, Ash was aware of the two disconnected parts of himself pulling in different directions.

There was Ash-from-before-the-brothel, who would have shoved Draven back a step, ruffled a hand through his close-cropped spiky hair just to piss him off, and come up with a careless quip to defuse the tension while silently wishing for the possibility of something more between them. Then, there was Ash-the-*veelaht*. Ash, the broken shell of a sex slave, who shrank back and let himself be handled by the larger male because that was what slaves *did*.

Both parts of Ash watched from a slight remove as Draven caged his body against the wall—the muscular Vithii still breathing as hard as though he'd been running for kilometers. Draven's head sagged until his forehead was nearly touching Ash's, his palms resting flat on the wall on either side of Ash's shoulders.

"Gods, Ash. I'm done with this," said the Vithii in a low voice. "*So* done with all of it. I can't do it anymore. I swore that if I found you alive, I'd stop hiding… and to hell with the consequences."

Air caught in Ash's throat as though his trachea had suddenly become lined with sandpaper. Part of him itched to get away. The other part itched to get closer.

"What are you talking about?" he heard himself ask in a hoarse voice, the words emerging flat and distant, as though they were coming to him through a tunnel.

Draven slumped forward even further, until his head rested against the juncture between Ash's neck and shoulder. Unease thrummed through Ash's body, an unpleasant crawling sensation that joined the cocktail of exhaustion and fast-souring adrenaline left over from his murder of the Adjunct and the guards.

"This," Draven whispered, one large hand cupping Ash's nape and tilting his head to the side. "I'm talking about this."

Lips and teeth closed around the tendon running up the length of Ash's neck. The skin there was raw and sensitive from the collar's constant rubbing. Ash froze—caught for a timeless instant between panic and an unexpected bolt of pleasure shooting from that single point of contact straight down to his balls.

Then panic won out, as every memory of being restrained by a Vithii male intent on fucking him piled onto his shoulders with the weight of an avalanche. Ash's vision whited out, his body acting on instinct as muscle memory from years of combat training kicked in without conscious thought.

He gripped his attacker's arm with his free hand and yanked sideways, taking the larger male off-balance as his right heel hooked the Vithii's left calf and swept his supporting leg out from under him. His opponent went down hard, with a surprised *oof*. When Ash's vision cleared, he was standing over Draven with the stolen sidearm he'd used to kill the guards aimed between his friend's amber-gold eyes. Draven looked up at him with his jaw hanging open in shock.

As the scene coalesced, Ash's heart skipped a beat. He jerked the muzzle up toward the ceiling. "*Shit!*"

Ash reflexively hurled the weapon away and took a step backward. When that didn't help clear the fog of dizziness and disorientation, he took another step, and another, until his aching back hit the wall and he slid down it.

Draven continued to stare at him, open-mouthed. The expression on his heavy features screamed *betrayal*. And Ash… just… *couldn't*.

Not now.

Probably not ever.

"Never do that again," he rasped. "I don't know why you came here in the first place, but I can't be what you want me to be, Draven."

Draven blinked at him, looking hurt, and lost, and oddly *young*. "What do you think I want you to be?" he asked slowly.

Ash didn't back down. Didn't look away, even though his eyes were burning. "Yours."

They watched each other warily across the gap of a couple of meters and two entirely different worlds. Ash's barely controlled panic was slowly giving way to post-crisis jitters and a throbbing headache, even though he knew objectively that the crisis had only just begun. He'd murdered a high-ranking Regime official in his own home, slaughtered his guards, and was holding the official's bondmate prisoner.

In the space of a single cycle, everything he'd worked and sacrificed and *bled* for over the past grueling months had gone off the rails, exploding into a spectacular fireball. Not only had he failed to keep his friends from doing exactly what he'd feared by coming after him; now he'd also destroyed any chance of gaining Jontalyss' help voluntarily.

All of it was ruined. Every injury, every trauma and humiliation he'd suffered at the Adjunct's hands... had been for *nothing*.

"Damn it, Draven," he whispered. "*Why*? Could you not trust me in this *one godsdamned thing*?"

"Trust you? Like you trusted us, you mean?" Draven shot back.

And then, before Ash's eyes, Draven shook his head sharply and pulled himself together. Ash could practically see him packing away all of the bullshit that wasn't important right now, and drawing pragmatism around himself like a cloak. It was just as well one of them was capable of that kind of self-discipline, Ash supposed, because *he* sure as hell wasn't.

"This situation isn't going to be salvageable," Ash said, even though that was the least useful contribution he could possibly have come up with. "We are *beyond* screwed after this."

Draven clambered to his feet, wincing a bit, and glared down at him. "The fuck you say." He scooped up Ash's discarded pistol and stuffed it into his belt. "Is the Adjunct dead?"

"Very."

Draven nodded. "Did he contact anyone about me before you put him out of my misery?"

"Yes." Ash let his eyes slip closed, wishing like hell that he could just find a dark, private hole somewhere and *sleep*. "He left a message for the Security Intendant to contact him in the morning and arrange for prisoner transport. As soon as the Intendant tries to call him back and gets no answer, this place will be swarming with Regime forces. And that's assuming we can get past the four guards outside without raising any alarms."

"What about the target? Where's she?"

Ash sighed and opened his eyes. "Handcuffed to a bed upstairs. No doubt she's rather cross with me at the moment, since I've just murdered her bondmate and left her *grei'kaapt*."

Draven raised an eyebrow at the 'handcuffed to a bed' part, but Ash couldn't even be bothered to rise to the bait.

"Okay," Draven said after a beat. "So I guess we'll have to take her with us as a prisoner. That should be fun. Now get your skinny ass up off the floor, so we can go collect her and get the fuck out of here."

He loomed over Ash, reaching a hand down as though offering to help him up. Ash glared at the appendage, feeling the crawling sensation beneath his skin return with a vengeance.

"*Don't. Touch me*," he grated. Draven froze for only a moment before backing off, leaving Ash no choice but to drag himself upright under his own steam. He did, swallowing a groan as every muscle and joint protested. "And my arse is not skinny," he added, once he was on his feet.

"Fuck off," Draven said. "It *is* skinny. You've lost weight. Also, your face is bleeding."

"Let it bleed," Ash snapped. "And allow me to clarify further. Don't touch me. Don't fuss over me. And don't look at me like some godsdamned stray puppy that I've just kicked in the ribs."

"How about I knock you right back down on your skinny human ass for acting like a prick, instead?" Draven muttered under his breath.

"Why not?" Ash asked in tired tones. "I've certainly had enough practice with that sort of thing recently."

Wisely—if somewhat surprisingly—Draven didn't offer anything further as Ash turned away and headed toward the upper levels of the house. Now he just needed to find out how badly fucked they were when it came to the Adjunct's newly minted widow. Jontalyss had hated Denrir as much as Ash had, it was true... but she'd also needed him. Now, Ash had ensured that she would forever be a social outcast within Vithii society.

As Draven had said, this next conversation was going to be *loads* of fun.

ELEVEN

Draven resolutely shoved everything away that wasn't directly related to getting him and Ash out of this mess alive. He cut off the human's attempts to talk calmly with the Adjunct's widow, in favor of pointing the blaster he'd taken from one of the guards at her head and telling her, "You're my prisoner. Do what I say or I'll blast your brains out."

"*Brilliant*," Ash muttered. "This whole thing just gets better and better."

The bondmate—Jontalyss—went very pale, but she didn't try to fight them when Ash unfastened the handcuffs from the bed frame. Draven was pretty sure she was exactly what she seemed—a spoiled upper class Vithii female who'd never been in a physical altercation in her life.

She did, however, balk at the door, looking over her shoulder at them with a pleading expression. "Is Denrir dead?"

There was no point in trying to hide it from her. "Yes."

"Please," she begged, "there's a case in the bathroom that I have to take with me."

Draven drew breath to tell her they didn't exactly have time for her to pack an overnight case, but Ash cut him off.

"The saliva vials?" the human asked.

Jontalyss nodded miserably. It took a moment for Draven to make the connection, but then understanding dawned. Her bonding with Lusivian had been a complete sham, and he'd been maintaining the ruse by giving her containers of his stored spit to use on her mating gland so she wouldn't start churning out *grei'kaapt* pheromones for the world to smell.

Fucking prophets… what an asshole.

"All right," Ash said, squeezing the bridge of his nose like his head pained him. "Look, the rest of the guards are outside, so we've got a few minutes to organize this. Let me get her some shoes, and some trousers to wear beneath that nightshirt. In fact, a pair of her shoes might work for me, too—certainly better than Denrir's or any of the guards' would. Jontalyss, tell me where the vials are stored and I'll get them."

Draven tapped his foot while Ash gathered the things he wanted. In the basement, the human had quickly changed from the stolen Vithii-sized clothing he'd been wearing when he freed Draven, to a shirt and loose trousers that actually fit him. But apparently, Lusivian hadn't allowed his *veelaht* any kind of footwear. Draven shoved his reaction to that particular bit of trivia down with all the rest of the stuff he couldn't deal with right now.

Ten minutes later, Ash was apparently happy with his preparations, which, did, indeed, bear a suspicious resemblance to an overnight bag. He was also wearing nondescript athletic shoes, which at least didn't flop around on his feet.

"Put these on," he said, handing a pair of casual trousers, socks, and shoes to Jontalyss.

She glared at both of them. "Turn around while I do."

Draven snorted in disbelief.

"Hypocrite," Ash said, holding her gaze steadily. "Shall I quote you what you told me the last time I asked you to get me some trousers to wear?"

She flushed copper and looked away.

Draven swallowed a growl at the continued delays, but he forced himself to speak calmly. "Trust me when I say that neither of us is interested in anything you have to offer."

Ash shot him a surprised glance before looking down quickly.

Jontalyss flushed even brighter and pulled on the pants, angling her body away from them. *Finally*, they all seemed to be ready, so Draven cuffed the woman's wrists behind her back. He also kept hold of one of her arms, and the three of them started back down toward the basement delivery entrance where he'd been brought in.

"Four guards are patrolling the perimeter outside," Ash warned, and Draven grunted in acknowledgement.

His duffel of weapons and equipment was no place to be seen, but he and Ash were armed with the blasters they'd taken from the downed guards, plus the compact lasers Ash had gotten from Denrir and Jontalyss earlier. Ash held the small bag he'd packed slung over his shoulder.

The human shot him a sidelong glance as they approached the large door. "What do you think? Let nature take its course?"

As usual, they were on the same page. "Sounds like a plan to me," Draven said, and swung the door open. Beyond it, all of the exterior lights were on, illuminating the area beyond the house with crisscrossing beams.

As they had both predicted, Jontalyss immediately started screaming for help. Within moments, two of the guards came running, and he and Ash shot them down. Jontalyss' screams grew shriller, and the other two followed soon after, only to join their friends in oblivion.

"Fucking amateurs," Draven muttered.

Ash gave him a pointed look. "They caught *you*, didn't they?"

Draven scowled at him. But since scowling at Ash had never worked in the history of *ever*, he quickly turned the expression on Jontalyss instead. "Thanks for the help and all, but you can shut up now," he told her, wiggling the blaster at her in warning.

She snapped her jaw shut, her eyes wide and frightened.

"It's a bit different when people die right in front of you, as opposed to dying at a distance because of things your bondmate has implemented as a matter of policy," Ash said in a mild tone.

"Denrir never—" she began in a scandalized tone.

"Killed anyone?" Ash finished, cutting her off. "Tell that to the half-dozen veelahts who came before me."

She opened and closed her mouth a couple of times. "But they were…"

"Human," Ash said. "Yes, I'm quite aware."

"You know who else is human?" Draven asked. "Isadora Martinez. But I guess she gets a special pass in your mind or something?"

Jontalyss flinched in his grip. *Hard.*

"No time for this shit now," Draven decided. "Come on. It's about half a klick to where the hovercar is hidden."

"And then?" Ash prompted. "*Please* tell me you have an exit strategy from this clusterfuck, Draven."

Draven blew out an unhappy breath through his nose. "That'll depend entirely on the others, and how pissed off they are at me. But either way, we need to lay low for twelve cycles or so. I'm guessing the safehouse locations aren't compromised? After you went AWOL, we weren't sure."

Ash's voice was tight. "Believe me, interrogation was the very last thing on the Adjunct's mind."

And that reply went straight down to simmer with the rest of the things Draven wasn't thinking about right now.

"Okay. There's a gap in the fence where we can get out. Come on. The farther away we are from here, the happier I'll be."

"Seconded," Ash whispered, barely audible.

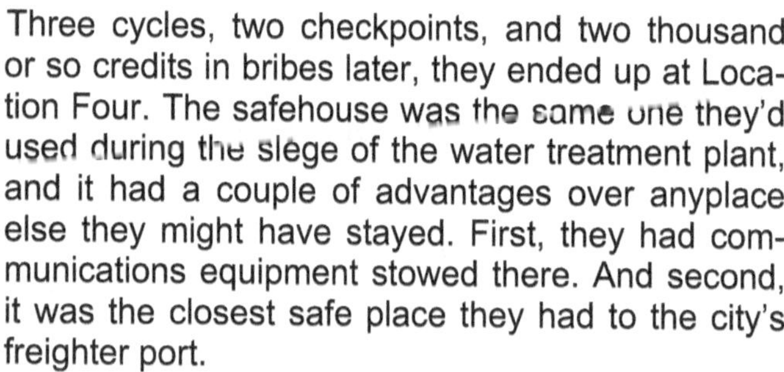

Three cycles, two checkpoints, and two thousand or so credits in bribes later, they ended up at Location Four. The safehouse was the same one they'd used during the siege of the water treatment plant, and it had a couple of advantages over anyplace else they might have stayed. First, they had communications equipment stowed there. And second, it was the closest safe place they had to the city's freighter port.

While Ash guarded Jontalyss, Draven commed Jonah.

"Tell me some good news, kid," he said bluntly.

"You first," Jonah shot back. "Did you get him? Is he okay?"

"He's here," Draven said, ignoring the last question for now.

An excited whoop came across the staticky connection.

"Enough of that," he said in a gruff tone. "What have you got for me?"

"Sorry," Jonah replied, getting himself under control again. "Okay, all I got since last time was an automated message. Just a string of numbers. You ready for them?"

Draven grabbed a pencil stub and a scrap of paper. "Yeah."

Jonah rattled off the numbers and he jotted them down.

"That help you at all?" Jonah asked.

"It does," Draven said. "We're good. Thanks, Jonah. I probably won't be contacting you again on this channel, so take care."

"You, too," Jonah said. "You and Ash both. Let me know if I can do anything in the future, okay?"

"Will do," Draven replied. "Out."

He glanced at Ash, who raised an eyebrow. "A ship's registration code?" the human asked.

Draven nodded. "Looks like Kade came through for us. Even after me and Skye stole his fighter so I could get here."

The human's other eyebrow joined the first.

"Don't give me that look. She took it back to the station afterward," Draven said dismissively.

Ash consciously smoothed his expression. "That's an interstellar commerce code."

He shrugged agreement.

Jontalyss sat huddled on the floor with her arms—now uncuffed—wrapped around herself. She'd been watching the exchange, looking from one to the other of them.

"You're taking me off-planet?" she asked in a small voice. "Look, you won't be able to get any kind of a ransom for me. My family doesn't have money anymore—we lost it during the last downturn. But Denrir does." She swallowed hard. "*Did.* It's mine now. I can pay you to let me go."

Draven felt his temper straining against the chains he'd slapped around it. "We don't want your fucking dirty Regime credits," he growled.

She curled tighter around herself, and Ash shot him an irritated glare.

"Then what *do* you want?" she asked.

"At a guess, my friends are trying to stage a college reunion for you," said the human. "Assuming we can get you off-planet in one piece."

✦

Before they left for the spaceport, Draven crouched in front of Jontalyss and met her gaze. She glared back at him with a mixture of fear and defiance.

"Here's how this is going to go down," he told her "I'm guessing you don't get out to the rougher parts of the Capital very much. But these days, security in those areas is a joke. People get robbed, beaten, and murdered all the time, and no one gives a shit."

She lifted her chin, trying for an air of bravado that was undercut by the faint trembling of her lower lip.

"But if you raise a fuss and do, by some miracle, manage to bring the authorities down on us," Draven continued, "I'll tell them who you are, and that you just murdered your bondmate in a jealous rage because he'd rather fuck a *veelaht* than fuck you. Then I'll show them your little spit collection as proof that he refused to touch you."

She went pale, and swallowed.

"Tell me exactly what's going to happen to me," she whispered.

"You'll get on a ship owned by a friend of mine, that I assume is going to Terra Nova," Draven told her.

"And when we get there," Ash cut in, "we sincerely hope that you'll agree to speak with your old friend Ambassador Martinez, to tell her firsthand what is happening on Ilarius."

She looked genuinely shocked. "Are you saying that… you really were after *me*? All of this was about *me*? Denrir, and… and the guards, and…"

"No," Draven said, looking at Ash. "Not all of it."

"Yes," Ash contradicted. His dark gaze turned stormy. "But believe me when I say, this was a far cry from the original plan."

Draven wanted to take up that gauntlet so badly he could taste it. But they had other things to worry about.

"It's time to leave," he said, rising from his crouch. "Remember what I said about the security forces, *Frey Lusivian*."

The drive to the spaceport was blessedly uneventful. Draven parked the old heap of a hovercar a short distance away and left the keys in the front seat. In this part of the city, someone would find a use for it before long. He took over guard duty for their prisoner as they walked toward the massive structure, since a Vithii male hustling a Vithii female along by the arm would raise far fewer eyebrows than a human doing the same.

A bored looking woman stood behind a battered information desk near the spaceport entrance. Draven rattled off the registration code Jonah had given him from memory, and the woman poked it into her terminal.

"Berth 37C," she said. "Departure is scheduled in thirty minutes, so you'd better hurry. I.D., please?"

Draven passed her a forged identichip that should be on file with Kade's shipping company. She scanned it and nodded him on.

He thanked her and headed toward Terminal C with the others in tow. Unlike the commercial passenger spaceport, the freighter port had minimal security these days. Much of the manpower that might once have been devoted here had been shifted to areas the Regime considered more pressing. It left a definite gap for exploitation, but the government was more concerned about bombs or attacks at places where they lived and worked than they were about freighters full of raw materials and trade goods.

That would change the moment anyone thought to stage a major attack here, but for now, it was decidedly useful. Especially since Draven and Ash happened to be acquainted with a crusty old asshole who actually *did* own controlling interest in a small interstellar trading fleet.

They reached the berth a few minutes later, to find the crusty old asshole in question leaning against the wall next to the umbilical gate. Kade was wearing his familiar dark flightsuit and worn leather jacket. He ran a critical eye over the three of them and pushed upright from his relaxed slouch.

"Well, son of a bitch," he said, his gray gaze centering on Ash. "I didn't want to believe it until I'd seen it with my own eyes. Hope you weren't expecting a tearful reunion, you crazy human bastard—because we need to get moving."

TWELVE

Ash poked at the place where his reaction to seeing Kade again should have lived. He felt that he should be more alarmed by the void he found there, but even alarm was beyond him right now, it appeared.

"Don't worry, old man. I'd sooner expect blood from a stone," he replied, reaching for an approximation of banter. "Kade, meet Jontalyss Lusivian. Jontalyss... this is another of my comrades, Ehkadian Finisterre."

Jontalyss maintained a stony silence, but Kade waved off the awkward moment. "Nice to meet you, I suppose—but there's no time for any of that shit right now. Come aboard."

He led them through the door and along the umbilical, shooting Draven a pointed look over his shoulder. "You owe me a new paintjob, by the way. Skye scratched the fighter's docking port all to hell when she got back to the station."

Draven scoffed "Pfft. Do me a favor. I saw the state of that docking port *before* we stole it." He sobered. "But, still... thanks for doing this, Kade."

Kade scowled. "Whatever. Like we were ever going to leave your stupid ass dangling over a cliff without throwing you a rope. *Idiot.*"

"Even so," Draven muttered. "Thanks."

Kade was spared having to come up with anything else dismissive to say when they arrived at the entrance to the freighter's bridge. Ash registered a couple of familiar faces among the crew—people he knew to be trusted long-time employees of Kade's.

"Are any of the others here?" he asked, because it seemed like a question that should be asked… even if the idea of having to face Ryder or Skye, in particular, made something twist unpleasantly in his gut.

Kade shook his head. "No. Pax and Nahleene are off doing their thing, and the others are planetside here on Ilarius, waiting to see if there's anything that needs to be done from this end."

"Not in the Capital, surely?" Ash asked, a thread of real alarm snaking through him as the phrase 'internment camps' flashed across his thoughts.

"Not in the city, no. They're holed up at the farmhouse."

He relaxed minutely.

Kade excused himself to check that everything was ready for takeoff. When he was satisfied, he gestured for them to follow him into the bowels of the aging freighter. Draven still had a grip on Jontalyss' arm, and Ash could see the poor girl shaking as he dragged her deeper into the unfamiliar ship.

"We're running with a skeleton crew," Kade said as he gestured them into a room at the end of the quiet corridor they'd been traversing. "Handpicked, obviously. They're all bunking in quarters at the other end of the wing. We should have complete privacy on this end."

The room was, in fact, set up as crew quarters—basic, but functional. Kade locked the door behind them, and Draven let Jontalyss go. She jerked away and backed up until her shoulders bumped against the far wall.

Kade glanced at her for only an instant before his steel-gray gaze swept over Ash, incisive and penetrating. "Well. You certainly look like shit right now, *leetha*. There's no doctor on board, but the sickbay is stocked and Rita knows some basic field medicine."

Leetha. Hearing the old, familiar nickname after the past few gut-wrenching weeks—and after the ruse he'd perpetrated on Kade and the others— made that earlier unpleasant twisting sensation return. He remembered his bemused reaction when Ryder had first compared him to the sleek Vitharan animal—not dissimilar to an Old Earthen antelope. The others had taken to teasing him with the name whenever he managed to emerge from a dangerous situation unscathed—*'like a leetha dodging a greilo-beast.'* Eventually, it had stuck.

Too bad he hadn't managed to evade the *greilo*-beast this time. Nope... this time, he'd been thoroughly mauled.

"It's fine," Ash said. "A few bruises are hardly our biggest concern. Have you been following the underground news and message boards? There's been a development."

Kade's features drew into hard, haggard lines, but Draven looked confused.

"What development?" Draven asked.

"Internment camps," Kade said tersely, "for *undesirable elements* within the Capital. I'm sure that doesn't require any further translation."

Draven cursed sharply.

The engines purred into life somewhere far beneath them. A few moments later, the ship started its slow ascent into the atmosphere. Jontalyss slid down the wall to sit on the floor, covering her face with her hands.

"Why am I here?" she asked. "Why are you *doing* this to me?"

Ash swallowed a sigh. "I already told you. We're taking you to see Isadora Martinez, in hopes that you'll speak with her about the conditions on Ilarius."

She dragged her hands down her face and glared daggers at him. "You're a filthy fucking liar, *veelaht*. You were playing me the whole time with your sob story about trying to help your family."

"Not really," Ash told her. "The only lie I told you was that I was there for the money. I was actually there for you. I got my parents off-planet years ago, for precisely the reasons I told you. And I *am* trying to help my family," he added, thinking of the two men in this room… the ones fighting for their cause on Maelfius… the others hidden away on the southern continent.

Again, he prodded at the place where his emotions should have been, and weren't.

Jontalyss surged to her feet. "Well, you just *killed* mine! As far as I'm concerned, you can go straight to hell, you dirty *whore*!"

Ash watched with distant surprise as Kade growled something under his breath and crossed the cabin in three long strides, crowding Jontalyss against the wall. He was also vaguely aware that Draven appeared to have grown six centimeters next to him, and was giving off roughly the same sort of vibes as a rabid attack dog.

Ash should… probably be doing something. Something like… trying to prevent either of them from further destroying whatever tiny thread of a connection he'd managed to forge with the Adjunct's bondmate. But it felt as though a weight were pressing down on him, sapping his strength—and the feeling had nothing to do with the faint increase in g-force as the ship climbed toward open space.

"All right—you listen to me, you spoiled little *trophy mate*," Kade was saying, his voice an angry rumble. "You want to talk about families? Mine was executed by the same government with whom you've been silently complicit all this time. Want to know why? They committed the *crime* of having a different political opinion. Does that bother you more than your husband's perversions, since my parents were Vithii rather than human?"

Jontalyss shrank back, but she had no place to go. "I—"

"*No*," Kade snapped. "You shut up and hear what I have to say. You want me to believe you're shedding tears over a sadistic bastard who'd rather screw a helpless sex slave than screw his bondmate? *Pull the other one.* The only tears you're shedding are for yourself. You're scared of being dragged away from your cushy, insulated little bubble, while the rest of us are out here *fighting for our lives.*"

"That's not—" Jontalyss began, only to cut herself off and change tack. "You're kidnapping me!"

"And you've spent *years* standing by while your piece-of-shit bondmate bought and sold human beings!" Kade snarled. "You're standing by while the government department he headed makes bioweapons and concentration camps to attack the very people who *built the damned colony you live on!*"

"Kade," Ash said quietly.

The Vithii cursed and pushed away from the wall where he had Jontalyss caged. The woman looked pale as a sheet.

"Is this cabin secure?" Ash asked.

"Yes," Kade bit out.

"Then leave her alone for a bit," he said. "Please. It's been… a very long day for everyone involved."

Kade shot Jontalyss a dark look. "*Prophets*. Do you even hear that, you self-centered little beast? Remember which person in this room wanted us to be *nice* to you. *Fine*. There are ration packs and water in the cabinet, and a latrine behind that panel." He gestured toward a small sliding door. "You'll be under continuous video surveillance, and there will be a guard on the door at all times. Try not to choke on your fucking *righteous indignation* while you're waiting. Like I said… we don't have a doctor on board."

With that, he stalked out. Draven hovered, as though he wasn't willing to leave Ash alone with her. Ash shot him a frustrated look before turning his attention to their prisoner.

"We'll talk when everyone's had some rest and a chance to cool down," he said. "You probably won't believe me, but I truly am sorry about… all of this."

With that, he turned and left, Draven following him like a very pissed-off shadow. The door closed behind them, the electronic lock engaging with a metallic clank. Draven drew breath to say something, but Ash cut him off.

"Don't."

Draven let the breath hiss out.

Kade strode ahead without waiting for them, walking off his anger. It was, quite honestly, the angriest Ash could ever remember seeing the man. Normally, Kade did *grumpy*. He did *snappish*. He didn't do… this. Whatever this was.

All of them were on edge. All of them except Ash, anyway, who still seemed to be stuck somewhere in the vicinity of *disconnected and off-balance*. Or at least, he was stuck there until Draven took a few long strides to get in front of him and raise his arm across the narrow corridor, barring Ash's way.

Ash came to an abrupt halt to avoid running into him. The crawling, twisting feeling inside him started up again, even as the heavy weight of fatigue pressed down on him from above.

"Was the word '*don't*' unclear somehow?" Ash asked pointedly, striving for coldness and barely achieving peevishness instead.

"Ash. We need to talk about what happened in that basement," Draven murmured, suddenly earnest.

"I have no idea what you're referring to," Ash told him, lying through his damned teeth.

"Yes, you do," Draven said evenly.

Ash arched an eyebrow and played dumb. "Oh? So sorry if I worried you with my act for the Adjunct. I was a little bit busy trying to ensure that he didn't just have you killed on the spot. And that I could get him alone somewhere, so I could kill *him*."

Draven waved the words away. "That's not what I meant, asshole. And you know it."

Ash gritted his teeth. "What, then?"

Draven held his gaze, and it was like torture not to look away. As if it had only now merited his notice, Ash realized how cold he felt. Were the ship's environmental systems set on energy saving mode, or something?

"I tried to put a Vithii love mark on your neck, Ash."

"And I believe I told you afterward never to do anything like that again," he said, fighting for an even tone with every syllable.

"You did," Draven agreed. "But we can't just... not talk about it. You did your level best to make me think that you were *dead*. And I swore that if I found you, I'd stop hiding how I felt..."

"This isn't the time or place to have this conversation," Ash said. "In fact, this is the polar opposite of the time and place to have this conversation. Draven, we're on an unarmed freighter, fleeing a murder scene with a kidnapping victim in tow."

"Yeah," Draven said. "We are. And we might get captured. We might die. Just like every other godsdamned day, right? Which isn't exactly the best way to convince me to put this off."

In desperation, Ash tried a different tactic. "I can't do this now, Draven. I need time first."

Some of his turmoil crept past his control and into his voice despite his best efforts, but maybe that was what ended up doing the trick. Draven gave him a searching look, and nodded unhappily.

"Time..." He sighed. "Okay. First we'll figure out how worried we need to be about getting blown up. But afterward, you come talk to me. Don't let it sit and fester between us, yeah?"

"Fine," Ash said, even though he had no intention of examining either Draven's actions in the basement, or his own reaction.

He looked past Draven to where Kade had stopped a couple dozen meters ahead of them. Out of earshot—probably. Draven followed his gaze and sighed, letting his arm fall to his side. Ash ducked past him without letting their skin brush, and strode toward Kade like a man on a mission. With a sigh, Draven followed him.

Kade gave them both a look. "If you two are done gazing into each other's eyes, maybe one of you would like to tell me how likely we are to find ourselves surrounded by security fighters on our way out of Ilarian-controlled space."

Ash waved a hand. "Don't look at me—I'm just along for the ride. Ask the person who actually thought this whole thing was a good idea."

Draven's lips curled down. "We should be okay to get out of Ilarian territory. The authorities will have found the bodies at the Adjunct's place by now, and I'm guessing a house like that had video surveillance in place."

"Yes, it did," Ash confirmed, realizing with an unpleasant jolt that he should have taken time to wipe the recordings before they left, and he hadn't. His wits had been too scrambled.

Draven only nodded, though. "So they'll know we took his bondmate with us, and they'll have footage of us that they can use to search for us with facial recognition software. Eventually, they'll track us to the freighter port, and probably to this ship."

"But that will take time," Kade finished for him. "So we're good on this end, but we'll be flagged for detention on the other end of the journey, most like-ly."

"Was this a regularly scheduled shipment to Terra Nova?" Ash asked. "Or did you have to pull it together specifically for us?"

"It's a regularly scheduled shipment, but it wasn't slated to go to Terra Nova," Kade said. "So they'd know something was off regardless, once we deviated from the filed flight plan."

Ash kneaded his forehead, trying to think. "All right. So we'll need to alter the ship's registration codes before we get into Terra Novan territory, or they're likely to detain and arrest us for extradition back to Ilarius before we have a chance to contact Ambassador Martinez."

"Sounds about right," Kade agreed. "We've got plenty of time, though. As long as the codes are switched out so it looks like the ship was supposed to be going to Terra Nova by the time we get there, we ought to be all right."

"If you get me a fleet roster to work from, I'll take care of it," Ash said, knowing that exhaustion was coming through loud and clear in his voice.

Kade nodded. "Like I said, there's time. A more interesting question is what the fuck we're sup-posed to do once we get there. Your target doesn't seem all that inclined to help us."

"No? Well, I wonder why that is?" Ash snapped. He dragged a hand down his face, winc-ing at the bruises he encountered. "I'll… work on her. Just avoid snarling in her face any more than the two of you already have."

"Spoiled children don't need more cosseting when they've had it all their damned lives," Kade shot back. "But it's your show, *leetha*. Do whatever the hell you want."

"It stopped being my show when Draven crashed in like a battering ram," Ash muttered, as though he hadn't already been falling to pieces before Draven showed up.

Draven scowled, but Kade only shrugged. "That part wasn't my idea. Of course, it also wasn't my idea when you went off-script and staged your fucking death so you could disappear off our radar. Now, come on. I want to be on the bridge when we leave Ilarian airspace. Not that we'll be able to do much about it if things go to shit, but I'd still feel better facing it head-on."

"Agreed," Draven said grimly.

Things have already gone to shit, Ash thought, but he only sighed and said, "Lead the way, in that case."

THIRTEEN

As predicted, the Ilarian authorities didn't manage to trace them in time to cause an issue with leaving the system. The freighter stayed on course until they were well out of range of the security zone, and then altered trajectory to head for Terra Nova. Despite the fact that this was the safest he'd been in weeks, Ash slept poorly that night.

The hired skeleton crew was utilizing smugglers' routes, which meant that they would be traveling for the better part of two days in normal space rather than using the wormhole gate situated nearest to Terra Nova. Aside from ensuring that the ancient freighter's ID codes were faked, Ash had nothing much to do with his time.

Once they were in uncontested space, Kade had taken a long look at Ash and forbidden him from touching the freighter's ID systems until he'd had at least ten cycles of sleep. That prospect should have sounded like nirvana. Instead, Ash tossed and turned in his borrowed quarters—dozing for a few minutes here and there, only to jerk awake from a tangle of dreams and memories.

The red light from the chrono stabbed at his eyes. The ship's engines, which had been faintly out of alignment ever since they'd left the upper atmosphere of Ilarius, grated on his nerves like fingernails against deckplates. His mental fog of exhaustion taunted him with the offer of sleep's oblivion, but the promised respite remained just out of reach.

Eventually, he sat up in disgust. "Lights, twenty percent."

The overhead lighting cycled up, illuminating the stark space. This cabin didn't even have a working computer console, so it wasn't as though he had anything here with which to distract himself—not unless he wanted to try disassembling the fucking chrono with no tools other than his fingernails.

He rested his elbows on his bent knees, staring balefully at the LED numbers taunting him until the idea of *chronocide-with-extreme-prejudice* began to sound legitimately appealing. Shaking his head in disgust, Ash pressed the heels of his hands into his gritty eye sockets. Red starbursts exploded behind his eyelids.

He was still sitting like that a few minutes later when the door chimed. He straightened, a jolt of worry rattling along his overtaxed nerves. It was the middle of ship's night and they were safe in uncontested space, far outside the borders of either Ilarian or Terra Novan territory. Ash had no idea what sort of emergency might be in progress, but he also couldn't think of any other reason why someone would be chiming him at this time of night—especially after Kade had more or less chased him off the control deck earlier.

He stood, bare feet padding across the chilly floor as he crossed to the door and palmed the lock. It slid open to reveal Draven's broad form silhouetted against the brighter lights of the corridor. Ash's stomach sank beneath the weight of a vague sort of dread.

"Oh. It's you," he said.

Draven brushed past him without waiting for an invitation, and ordered the lights to fifty percent before rounding on him with a determined expression carved into his broad features.

"Do come in," Ash said pointedly. "Make yourself right at home. Don't mind me."

He could guess why Draven might show up like this. And it wasn't something Ash felt remotely prepared to deal with right now.

"I told you to come talk to me. But you didn't," Draven said, confirming Ash's fears. "The computer flagged it for me when you raised the lights, so I knew you were awake. I figured now was as good a time as any to come here and hash this out."

Ash stared at him. "It's oh-two-hundred ship's time, and you're *cyber-stalking* me while I sleep? Really, Draven?"

Shock of shocks, Draven didn't back down.

"What are you bitching about? You're not asleep now, are you? Besides, I already tried *giving you space*, or whatever the fuck humans call it when you let shit simmer away in the background instead of dealing with it properly. You could've come to me on your own so we could talk about what happened in the basement of that house, but you didn't. So I'm coming to you. We can do this the easy way or the hard way—that's your choice. But one way or another, we're going to have it out. Right here, right now."

With that, he tossed three items onto the foot of the bed. Ash's gaze fell on a pair of handcuffs, a key, and a tube of medical-grade lube. His entire body went cold, an abrupt fight-or-flight response urging him to either lunge for the nearest thing that could be used as a weapon, or turn and flee through the door behind him.

But both of those impulses were ridiculous. Not to mention unnecessary, despite what his fucked-up instincts were screaming at him. Ash took slow, deep breaths, refusing to become the frightened beast that the Adjunct had tried so hard to turn him into. He leveled a dangerous glare at Draven.

"On the scale of 'one' to 'funny,' this rates lower than a zero. Now *get*. The *fuck. Out*." Prophets. He barely recognized his own voice. But at least it wasn't shaking—small mercies.

Draven crossed his arms stubbornly and didn't budge. "The cuffs aren't for you, idiot. They're for me."

Ash blinked, replaying the words to confirm he'd heard them properly. "*What*?"

A low noise rolled up from Draven's chest. "You've been letting Vithii perverts hurt you, telling yourself the whole time that you were actually the one in charge, because you were on a *mission*." Draven spat the last word out like a curse. "But at some point, you lost control of things. It stopped being a trick you were playing on them, and it started being real."

"*Fuck you*," Ash hissed. "You know damned well why I did what I did. You knew what was at stake the whole time, even if you've been judging me for my actions *relentlessly* for months now!"

"I don't give a shit what was at stake!" Draven snapped. "You forced the rest of us to stand by twiddling our thumbs while you got the crap beaten out of you, over and over. Beatings and… *worse*."

"'*Worse*'? You can't even say the word aloud, can you?" Ash taunted. He could feel a frightening pit of ugliness welling up inside his soul… threatening to overflow and flood this tiny box of a room, drowning a man Ash cared for in a sea of vitriol he didn't deserve.

"While you were *raped*," Draven said very clearly and distinctly. "You forced me to stand by twiddling my thumbs while I knew you were being *raped*, and I couldn't do a *godsdamned* thing to stop it."

A strange lightheadedness threatened to overcome him at hearing the statement laid out so starkly.

"It's not rape when you agree to let it happen," Ash said. The darkness inside him rose a little higher, demanding release.

Draven's lips curled back in a snarl. "Oh? Is that right? Then prove it. The handcuffs are right there. Put them on me; I won't stop you. It's my idea. I'm *agreeing to let it happen*, and I can't do much to you if I'm chained to a bulkhead strut, now can I? But you can do whatever you want to me. You won't fucking *talk* to me, so maybe you'd rather do this instead."

Ash stared at him. Something awful writhed inside him, as though desperate to escape.

"Never give someone that kind of control over your body," he said hoarsely, trying to hold everything inside. "You have *no conception* of the things a person can do to another person when they're helpless."

Draven shrugged, and started unfastening the closures of his shirt. "Yeah? Well, *I don't care*. You won't hurt me. Not in any way that matters."

The darkness surged, roiling within its banks. "I could."

"But you won't." Draven's words were supremely confident.

Ash stared at him. "Won't I?"

Draven tossed his shirt on the floor and held Ash's eyes. "Nah. And even if you did… well… it wouldn't exactly be the first time someone's hurt me. Probably not the last, either."

That odd sense of disconnectedness slid over him again. At the same time, Ash became abruptly, viscerally aware that they were both standing in the small room half-clothed—him wearing nothing but a pair of low-slung sleep pants, Draven in standard issue crew trousers and deck boots.

"You're a fool," Ash heard himself say. "You think you want this? Fine. Strip, then. All of it."

He had some vague notion of pushing Draven until Vithii male dominance instinct kicked in, and… well… he wasn't sure what he expected to happen then, exactly. Draven might adopt the role of good-natured beta male to Hunter and Kade's growly alphas in their dysfunctional little family of choice. But in all other ways, he was about as naturally submissive as an Old Earth grizzly bear. And the faster Ash could prove that point to him, the faster this—*whatever* the fuck this was—would be over.

Ash desperately needed to hide away and lick his wounds in private. He needed to get control of the pit of angry bitterness currently threatening to swallow him whole. What had *happened* to him? What part of him had become broken and twisted to the point that this situation was sending the first trickle of genuine sexual desire Ash had experienced in months down to his cock? For fuck's sake, he shouldn't be *getting off* on this—on seeing his *friend* pretending to submit to him, against every instinct that Vithii males possessed.

Ash knew he should put a stop to this sham immediately. But instead, he continued to watch as more and more bronze skin was revealed to his gaze. In moments, Draven stood completely naked in front of him, his dick half-hard and his gaze silently challenging.

"Take the handcuffs," Ash said, still trapped in that strange sense of not being truly present for what was happening. "Cuff your wrists behind your back and kneel on the floor."

Prophets, what was he *doing*? And what was *Draven* doing, going along with him like this? Draven awkwardly snapped on the cuffs onto his wrists and knelt, his eyes sparking copper fire the whole time. Still watching the scene as though from a slight remove, Ash stepped forward until he was looming over his longtime comrade.

"I'm going to show you why this can never work, Draven," he said. "I know you think you can just pretend your instincts don't matter, but I guarantee that half a cycle from now, you'll be resenting the hell out of me for what I'm about to do to you."

Draven looked up at him. "You're wrong. I'm not the one who needs to learn a lesson from this. You are. So stop flapping your lips and take control. That's what you want, isn't it? To take charge? Get yourself a little bit of payback?"

"No," Ash said, almost absently. "It *really* isn't." Still feeling more like a spectator to what was happening than a participant, he dragged the stretchy waistband of the sleep pants he was wearing down just far enough to free his cock. "You think you need to prove something? Then suck me. And if I feel so much as a hint of teeth, I guarantee you won't like the consequences."

Draven knelt in front of the human he'd pined after for years. He could see the broken edges lurking behind Ash's dark gaze, ready to slice deep and draw blood. For the first time since the incredibly awkward conversation he'd had with Pax on the lunar outpost, Draven felt like he understood what the cyborg had been trying to tell him about Vithii sexual dominance instincts.

By rights, Ash's attempts to humiliate and goad him should be maddening. In reality, all he could think about was how much easier it would be to take care of the human and prove to Ash that he wasn't in danger if his damned hands weren't cuffed behind him. But Draven's first instinct had been right. This was how it needed to go down, at least for now.

Instead of worrying about the cuffs, he focused on the pulse-pounding realization that he was here, with another male, in safe and private surroundings for the next few cycles as they cruised through unclaimed space. For the first time in his life, he was about to be true to his own nature—and screw the consequences.

Ash's face was pale beneath his olive skin, but he'd crowded into Draven's space and pulled his strange human cock out like a challenge, daring Draven in so many words to back down from it. *Ridiculous*. As if Draven hadn't spent nights upon nights fantasizing about his mouth traveling over every square centimeter of Ash's skin. Maybe this wasn't the place he'd pictured starting his exploration, but he sure as fuck would have ended up here eventually.

He nuzzled into the delicate skin at the crease of Ash's hip, noting with interest that the human's groin was completely hairless. Most of the men in the holovids Draven had watched in recent days were also smooth-skinned, but he knew that wasn't a human male's natural state. Draven wondered if Ash removed his body hair out of personal preference, or because the assholes he'd sold himself to expected it of him.

Someday, maybe he'd ask.

Now, though, he dragged his lips further down the defined V he was exploring. Draven breathed in, and felt Ash's breath catch above him in reaction. There was no rush of resulting pheromones—or at least, none that Draven's body was designed to detect. Ash just smelled like… Ash. And, honestly? That was all Draven needed right now.

"Stop fucking stalling," Ash rasped.

Callused fingers tangled in Draven's hair and tightened. He'd always kept his hair close-cropped, for practicality more than anything else. It was too short to allow an opponent to get a serious grip during a fight, but Draven wasn't fighting now. Ash managed to trap enough of the short spikes between his fingers to tug Draven's head where he wanted it, and the pull against his scalp felt… surprisingly good.

And then Ash was holding his dick in his free hand, rubbing the tip against Draven's parted lips in insistent demand. Human cocks were… different. Odd-looking when they were soft, unexpectedly stiff and unmoving when they were aroused. Ash's was somewhere in between the two states, the shiny head just beginning to peek out of its foreskin.

Draven licked the glans, and the hand in his hair tightened until his scalp tingled. Mentally replaying as much of the relevant holovid footage as he could remember, he closed his lips around the entire head and ran his tongue around its contours. Ash's breath stuttered again, the small sound drawing a decidedly possessive rumble from Draven's chest.

Searching for the things that seemed to draw the most reaction, Draven alternated licking and sucking. Gradually, the prick in his mouth swelled to full hardness. Ash let go of the base and used his grip on Draven's hair to pull him closer, driving more of his length past Draven's lips.

Draven concentrated on keeping his teeth covered and not choking as Ash took control of his head. As Draven could easily have predicted, the human was far from brutal about it. The practice was unfamiliar, and not something he himself would enjoy receiving beyond a bit of light teasing and licking, maybe. But listening to Ash's breathing grow ragged... feeling Ash's dick thicken and pulse against his tongue... *yeah*. Those were both things that Draven could get behind.

In fact, he was surprised at how much this was affecting him. His goal tonight had been simple. Come here. Prove to Ash that he was serious, and that Ash didn't need to worry about his safety. Prove to himself that he could offer himself to another male, and no deadly lightning bolts would rain down on his head as a result of divine retribution from the gods.

Simple.

Frankly, he'd assumed the threat would be enough to convince Ash to talk to him, instead. For that reason, he hadn't devoted all that much thought to what his own body's reaction might be, but in the back of his mind he hadn't expected to get much out of it physically. It was all supposed to be for Ash. What *Ash* needed. Not what Draven's cock needed.

None of which explained why Draven's cock was starting to ache, growing thick and heavy between his legs as the tip writhed and stretched, *seeking*. And that was… a bit awkward, actually. Vithii dicks tended to be pretty single-minded when it came to their goal of being buried inside a nice warm, tight passage. But *his* dick needed to get over itself, since it wasn't going to be getting what it wanted tonight. Or possibly for a very long time afterward.

Draven hadn't just been researching homosexual sex in his spare time. He'd looked into the aftermath of sexual trauma, too. And while the prophets knew he didn't claim to understand how Ash's mind worked—or any human's, really—he'd be damned if he *ever* pressured Ash to let himself be fucked if he didn't want it.

Current appearances aside, tonight wasn't about sex at all. It was about trust. Aside from a handful of occasions as a teenager when Draven had stumbled through an unfulfilling fuck with a willing Vithii female as a way to direct suspicion away from his dangerous proclivities, Draven's prick had survived just fine without sex. It wasn't going to shrivel up and fall off simply because Ash didn't want it knotting his ass.

But, *damn*, the ache in it was starting to get distracting. And now he was beginning to release a dribble of slick—the natural lubricant that Vithii males produced when they were aroused, in preparation for intercourse. Prophets, what the hell was wrong with him?

He tried to focus on Ash, getting his tongue back in the action and adding more suction on the upstroke. There was no question that Ash was affected by what was happening, but Draven wasn't sure the sounds slipping past the human's control were really what you'd call *pleasure*. Though the angle was awkward, Draven opened his eyes and tried to get a good look at Ash's face, to gauge his expression.

Ash's dark gaze was hooded, and as Draven had feared, he appeared more like a man looking into his own private hell than one about to get his brains sucked out through his prick. Their eyes met and held. Draven wasn't sure what Ash saw in his expression, but in the next instant, Ash shoved him backward with enough force that Draven had to catch himself with his cuffed hands.

"*Fuck*," Ash snarled, stumbling back a step and hastily dragging his pants up to cover himself.

FOURTEEN

"Problem?" Draven asked in a mild tone—one that clearly conveyed an undercurrent of sarcasm. Because Ash might be a godsdamned basket case right now, but Draven sure as hell wasn't going to start treating him any differently than usual because of it.

"Yes, there's a bloody *problem*," Ash snapped. "No way is that the first time you've sucked a cock. Where the fuck did you pick up something like that, when you've been playing the clueless, closeted virgin ever since I've known you?"

Draven stared at him, blinking. "Seriously? *This* is what you're worried about? I'm surprised to hear that this comes as news to a techworm, but there are *videos on the hypernet*, you moron."

Ash's mouth opened and closed several times. It was actually kind of fascinating to watch. Eventually, he found words.

"I swear to the gods, Draven—if you've compromised my security systems so you could watch gay porn, I will personally tip you out of the nearest airlock," he finally managed.

"Could you maybe not insult my fucking intelligence while I'm at eye level with your dick?" Draven shot back, conveniently ignoring his own *moron* comment earlier.

Ash was still staring at him. "I cannot *believe* you've been watching hairless twinks deep-throating each other while we're neck deep in a civil war." He frowned, his sculpted human features hardening. "I damn well hope you weren't expecting reciprocity."

Draven snorted in derision. "Don't do me any favors, asshole. I've got no interest in standing around with my knot waving in the breeze like a flag."

That much was the unvarnished truth. Nothing was worse than popping a knot outside of a warm, welcoming body. It was a fucking miserable feeling, and you were stuck with it for what felt like forever until it went down on its own—usually in a cycle or so. Every pubescent Vithii boychild with a functioning right hand learned that lesson fairly early on, and Draven had been no exception.

But Ash's stony expression didn't crack. "Good. Because that won't be happening. *Ever*."

Draven sighed and jutted his chin toward the tent beneath Ash's waistband. "You didn't finish. Look… I'll admit I came here to make a point, but I also want this to be good for you, if we can manage to stop sniping at each other that long."

Ash shook his head slowly, still wearing that carefully blank face. "That's generous of you, I suppose, but it's a waste of your time. I won't be able to come that way. I only climax from one thing these days, and as far as I'm concerned, if that thing never happens again it'll still be too soon."

Draven's brow furrowed as he tried to untangle that statement.

"I don't understand," he said eventually.

"That's right," Ash agreed, "you don't. And unless you want me to chain you to that bulkhead strut and show you exactly what I'm talking about, you'll agree to stop chasing after something that could never work, and get the *fuck* out of my quarters."

"Then you'd better man up and show me, because I'm not leaving," Draven said stubbornly. "In case it escaped your attention, you just shoved your cock down my throat, and not only am I not in the throes of any Vithii male dominance shit—I actually kind of enjoyed it."

Ash went very still. "Uncuff yourself and get out of my room," he said.

"No," Draven shot back, rising to his feet as smoothly as he could with his arms still confined. He felt behind him for the key on the bed and unlocked one of the wrist bracelets, leaving the other one attached. "I already told you—I'm giving you two choices, Ash. You either talk to me properly, or you shackle me to whatever you think is sturdy enough to make you feel safe around me, and you fuck me. One of those two things is happening. You have to pick which one."

Something dangerous had been roiling behind Ash's gaze since the human had ordered him to kneel. It was only because Draven was watching him so closely that he saw the moment that darkness snapped its chains. One moment, the human was as cold and unmoving as marble, standing a couple of meters away with his fists clenched by his side. The next, he was in Draven's face, his expression the same shade of tortured it had been when Draven was sucking him earlier.

"Gods*damn* you, Draven," he grated, his voice about as far from its usual smoothness as it was possible to get. "Why can't you just *leave this alone*?"

"Because it's hurting you," Draven said simply. "And I need that to stop."

Ash shoved him, the bed cutting Draven off at the knees so that he fell back on it in a clumsy sprawl. "You don't understand," Ash said, still in that sandpaper voice. "You don't know what you're asking for."

Draven wasn't sure if he was referring to the sex, or their relationship, or what. But he let himself be manhandled without comment, since it was pretty clear that under duress, Ash had decided to go for option B. He let Ash rip the handcuff key from his fingers and toss it onto the floor next to the bunk. Then he let the human drag his arms over his head and run the chain of the cuffs through one of the holes drilled in the durasteel structural beam to reduce its weight, before snapping the loose bracelet around his free wrist again.

Ash was breathing hard when he straightened—two high points of color tingeing his cheekbones, even though the rest of his face had a grayish cast beneath the cabin's unflattering strip lighting. It looked like Draven had been right; the two of them were done talking. The little tube of medical-grade lubricant had fallen off the bed when Ash shoved Draven onto it, but now he scooped it up and twisted the cap off without comment.

Draven held his burning human gaze, unblinking, as Ash shoved his leg to the side and forced a slick finger into his ass without either gentleness or finesse. And… yeah. It kinda sucked. The intrusion burned like hell, hovering just on the wrong side of pain.

"Tell me to stop," Ash snarled.

Draven continued to hold his gaze. "No."

Ash pulled out and added a second finger, still looking as though he was staring his own damnation in the face. The burn intensified, and Draven had to cover a small wince. Prophets knew he hadn't expected to *enjoy* this, but he was working very hard now not to think too closely about how many times Ash must have been subjected to a far rougher version of this treatment. The realization made Draven feel distinctly ill.

Presumably, some humans did this kind of shit by choice, and Draven couldn't claim to understand what was going on with that. There was the prostate thing he'd read about, sure—but, *ugh*. Who cared, when getting access to the damned thing was so uncomfortable?

Still, it didn't matter… though it did make Draven more certain than ever that this kind of sex with Ash would be out of the picture forever. True—it was far from the worst discomfort Draven had ever experienced—very far from it, in fact. But he wasn't about to do anything sexual to Ash that hurt him. *Ever*. Not even if it only hurt him a little bit.

Speaking of Ash, the human was scissoring his fingers now, stretching Draven's ass until the ring of muscle guarding it stopped clenching and started fluttering instead. A strange little jolt of… *something*… zinged up from the intrusion to coil at the base of his spine, tingling. A moment later, it happened again—distracting Draven from the burning stretch until Ash added a third finger and pressed back in.

He couldn't suppress a low hiss at that, but then the tingling was back, and the burning started to subside by slow degrees as his muscles stopped resisting and began to give way.

Ash bared his teeth in an ugly expression.

"*Tell me to stop, damn it.*"

"No," Draven repeated, wishing there was some easier way for Ash to fight his demons than… whatever was happening right now.

He'd never seen the human's face look like this before, and he never wanted to again. Not for the first time, a desire washed over him to somehow go back in time and stop all of this mess with the Regime before it ever got started. The Adjunct was dead. No one could punish him now. Draven had always hated the Premiere for what he'd done to Ilarius, but that hatred had never before felt so *personal*.

Ash had broken something inside himself while fighting against the Regime's evils, and Draven wanted nothing more than to break the Premiere, in turn—with his bare hands, if necessary.

In the midst of his distraction, Draven had nearly missed the way his body opened to accommodate Ash's assault, the burn nearly lost beneath the tingling jolts bouncing back and forth along his nerves. In fact, he felt oddly empty when Ash pulled out again, this time so he could squeeze more lube into his palm.

Draven's gaze fell to Ash's groin and caught there when the human once again pulled down the waist of his loose pants, exposing his cock. As before, he was somewhere between limp and erect, and he fisted himself with a look of determination laced with anguish—spreading the lube over his length and bringing his dick to something approaching full hardness.

"I'm not a fucking *top*," he spat. "I've never had any godsdamned desire to be a top. And since bottoming is ruined for me now, I don't know what the hell that makes me these days. Nothing, I suppose. It makes me *nothing*."

Draven was silent, letting the bitter words pour over him without trying to argue or shut them down. Ash settled between Draven's legs, hitching them up roughly until he was lined up at Draven's opening. He didn't meet Draven's eyes as he spoke.

"I don't understand why you're doing this. By the time you leave this room, you're going to despise me. And you'll be right to do so."

That one, Draven couldn't let pass.

"No, Ash," he said quietly. "You're wrong."

Then, he swallowed a gasp as Ash clenched his jaw and thrust in, his human cock feeling impossibly larger than his fingers had. The burn was back, more intense than ever—but so were the deep, ever-spreading tingles.

"Sure about that, are you?" Ash said through gritted teeth.

"Completely," Draven told him.

"*Godsdamn you,*" Ash hissed, pulling back and thrusting in again until he was completely buried. Draven felt the strange hanging pouch of skin that housed the human's testicles slap against the flesh of his ass.

The intrusion still felt decidedly unpleasant. And it continued to feel decidedly unpleasant each time Ash repeated the sharp movement in and out… right up until he shifted his grip on Draven's hips as though to gain better purchase. The angle of the next thrust changed minutely, and starbursts erupted in Draven's vision. His breath lodged in his throat, nearly choking him as the nebulous tingling in the base of his spine exploded outward in a violent ripple of liquid heat.

His jaw fell open, but there were no words behind the gesture. Any that he might have come up with, like '*what the fuck was that*' or '*why didn't you warn me about this, you asshole,*' disappeared under the next assault of sharp, nearly painful pleasure.

Draven's dick surged awake with no warning, full and aching, twisting in search of a home that didn't exist. A fresh trickle of slick welled up from the slit and dripped down his length. Ash seemed oblivious to the effect he was having, still too caught up in fighting his own demons.

"*Ash*," Draven choked, as fresh waves of heat washed over him, threatening to drown him.

"Shut *up*," Ash ground out. "Unless it's to tell me to stop, *don't fucking talk to me.*"

Draven snapped his jaw shut, for fear that Ash would follow through on the implied threat and stop doing what he was doing. He slammed his eyelids shut, too, because everything was starting to spin in a dizzying, overwhelming blur as the human pounded into him faster and harder.

Closing his eyes had the unfortunate side effect of focusing his attention more wholly on what his body was feeling, and *that* turned out to be a really bad idea. Ash hadn't so much as brushed against Draven's traitorous cock, and yet the damned thing was twitching and pulsing with every fresh wave of pleasure from his even more traitorous ass. Damn it all… much more of this, and he was going to—

Before Draven could finish the half-formed thought, Ash plowed into him again and something inside him tipped over the edge, overflowing its bounds. Draven cried out hoarsely and convulsed, the metal cuffs biting into his wrists as the chain clattered noisily against the heavy support strut. His dick jerked and spilled, spurting hot ropes of semen over his chest and stomach until Draven was sure he'd pass out from the intensity of the unexpected orgasm.

He'd never come like that in his fucking *life*, and it was so good… so overwhelming. He didn't want it to ever stop, because when it stopped—

Ash had frozen in place above him, going utterly motionless when the choked cry of release passed Draven's lips. Draven tried to blink him into focus, but the human's outline stayed blurry. Their ragged breathing echoed in the small room, out of sync. The intense spasms of pleasure slowly ebbed, replaced by a new pressure building in Draven's cock as his knot filled.

A low, distraught noise escaped his shattered control, and he shivered, a cold feeling radiating outward from his exposed knot to skitter up his spine, gooseflesh rising in its wake.

"*Shit*," Ash cursed, still breathing hard.

Draven could feel the cock inside his ass going limp, even as his own filled and ached. He shuddered harder, partly because of the horrible chill, and partly at the feeling of sudden emptiness as Ash slid out of his body.

Stupid, he berated himself. *Stupid, clueless idiot…*

He tried to steel himself, preparing for the humiliating discomfort to come. Draven knew he needed to downplay it; he had to hide from Ash how much this was affecting him. He drew breath to ask the human to uncuff him, not sure if he'd even be able to do up the fastening of his trousers for the tortuous walk of shame back to his own quarters—but hoping he'd at least be lucky enough not to meet anyone else on the way.

But Ash didn't rise to leave the bunk. Instead, a harsh noise tore from his throat, and he lowered his body until it pressed on top of Draven's, trapping his aching knot between the heated skin of their hard-muscled stomachs. It wasn't what Draven needed, exactly—but it was more than he'd expected. It was warm and protected, at least. It was *something*.

"I'm sorry," Ash whispered, sounding suddenly young and lost. "I didn't... think that would happen. Not to you."

"Ash," Draven began, feeling just as lost all of the sudden.

"No—don't," Ash warned.

"But I need—" he tried, feeling everything he'd ever wanted to say to the human welling up in him at once.

"*Don't*," Ash said, more harshly this time. "I swear, Draven—if you start in with the fucking Vithii pillow talk, I will walk out that door and leave you chained to the wall with your knot hanging out in the cold."

Draven clenched his teeth to keep anything else from slipping out. It was difficult. Shockingly so. The one time his bloody biology demanded that he confess to his mate all the important words and feelings that were too difficult to say in the normal course of things, Ash refused to hear them. Instead, it was Ash who started talking, the words emerging in fits and starts at first, then gradually gaining steam.

In low tones, Ash described the humiliation of being betrayed by one's body due to a quirk of biology... the way Denrir Lusivian always laughed uproariously at the sight of Ash spilling all over himself after being beaten and knotted—asking Ash if he liked it, if he was enjoying himself. He talked about the casual cruelty leveled at *veelahts* and *seelahts*, the culture of fear reinforced by the gleeful sharing of stories that might or might not be true.

'So-and-so just killed his seelaht last week, did you hear? She tried to escape, apparently. After the guards caught her, he strapped her down so tight she could barely wiggle and forced a spider gag into her mouth so she couldn't bite him. Then he fucked her throat until he popped a knot inside her mouth and suffocated her. Such an intriguing idea, don't you agree, cur?'

'Oh, have you heard? My old friend General what's-his-name accidentally turned his latest veelaht into a mental vegetable by hitting him in the head too hard. The servants gave the pathetic beast a couple of days to bounce back—but he just kept drooling and pissing himself, so they snapped his neck and threw the body out in the barrens for the scavengers to eat.'

Ash went on to describe the constant battle to dissociate mentally from the physical pain and mental trauma, while maintaining enough awareness to understand and remember any bit of important information that Lusivian might let slip in an unguarded moment. For the first time, Draven began to truly understand the nature of the razor-thin tightrope Ash had walked for months—playing a role where any mistake could be deadly as he tried to milk the Adjunct for useful Regime intel, while simultaneously cultivating an emotional connection with the Adjunct's bondmate in secret.

Draven's hands twitched with the urge to wrap his arms around Ash's shoulders and protect him from the world. His lips and tongue burned with the need to tell the human that he was loved… that he was worth more than the mission… that Draven would never let him be in such a position ever, ever again.

Hormones, he told himself over and over. *It's the fucking hormones; just hold on until your knot starts to deflate. Don't scare him away.* Because Draven had no doubt that if he let a single word slip out, if he made a single move to fight against the handcuffs holding his arms above his head, Ash would make good on his threat and flee.

And indeed, after the longest cycle of Draven's life, when his thrice-damned cock finally got over itself and his knot softened, Ash was up as if the touch of Draven's skin against his burned him—scrubbing at his hands and dick with a steri-wipe from the box on the table near the bunk; pulling up his pants and throwing on a too-large shirt. His brown gaze was distant and dazed as he retrieved the key from the floor, and he didn't look at Draven's face for even an instant as he pressed it into Draven's hand.

"This never happened, and it *won't* be happening again. *Ever*," Ash said without looking back, as he paused just inside the doorway. Then, he fled the room, leaving Draven naked on the bunk, growing sticky with his own spilled slick and semen… still cuffed to a strut.

Draven sighed and carefully eased the key into the lock on his opposite wrist, popping it open. "Yeah… not like this, it bloody won't be," he muttered.

FIFTEEN

Going to Kade's quarters for relationship advice was quite possibly the most moronic thing Draven had ever done. Seriously—it was on pretty much the same scale as going to Ryder for sympathy over a hangnail, or visiting a *greilo*-beast for advice on vegetarianism.

But Draven had come to an uncomfortable revelation not too long ago, namely that his deep, dark secret hadn't been a secret to any of his friends for a very long time… if ever. Ash was in pain. Ash needed help. That meant Draven's fears and insecurities about his own nature didn't matter. His worries about how the others would react didn't matter. Nothing mattered except fixing whatever it was that had broken inside the human during his stint as a sadist's plaything.

He buzzed the door, figuring that Kade would probably be up at this crazy hour thanks to his need for a neurotonin fix. The addiction his jailers in the Ilarian prison had gifted him with was a merciless mistress, and it didn't give two shits about his sleep schedule.

A moment later, the door slid open, revealing Kade wearing the drawn expression universal to addicts in the small cycles of the morning.

"I need help," Draven said without preamble.

Kade's brows drew together in confusion. And in his defense, that wasn't something Draven said to people very often, so maybe Kade's reaction was understandable. Then the older man's nostrils flared, scenting the air. His steel-colored gaze raked up and down Draven's body once.

"Well, *shit*," he said. "Because *this* is exactly what I needed on top of everything else tonight." He jerked his chin toward the interior of his cabin. "You'd better come inside."

From anyone else, such a greeting might've been off-putting. From Kade, it was pretty much the same greeting Draven would have expected if he'd showed up with news of a database error or a blown generator in the ship's electrical system.

He went inside.

Kade waved him to the room's single chair and sat on the edge of the rumpled bunk across from him. "I have two questions," he said, once Draven was settled. "One—who fucked who, and two— what the hell made you think this, of all *possible* times, was the right moment to finally plant your damned flag?"

Draven tried to ignore the hot flush of embarrassment crawling up his neck to stain his cheeks. "Before I answer that, I need to know if I can speak about this plainly, or if I need to dress it up for you at all. It's not something Vithii really… discuss openly, if you take my meaning."

Kade met his gaze head-on. "*Fucking prophets*. Seriously, Draven? Don't talk to me about societal norms. I've been impotent ever since the guards in the Capital prison pumped me full of neurotransmitter antagonists. If a medical specialist told me, 'We can fix your dick, but it will only work properly if you screw men,' I'd probably go for it at this point. Just answer the damned questions."

"He fucked me," Draven said. "I showed up at his quarters and told him he had two choices—talk to me properly, or handcuff me to the bed so he didn't have to worry about me hurting him while he did whatever he wanted to me. I… didn't really expect him to go through with it."

Kade continued to stare at him, until Draven wondered how the man could go so long without blinking.

"*Amazing*. You've had his cock in your ass, but it's like you don't even know him," Kade said eventually.

Draven bristled. "I know him well enough to be able to see when something inside him is shattered into pieces! What the hell am I supposed to do? Let him stew in his own juices until he convinces himself we'd be better off without him, or some shit like that?"

The other man snorted. "The bastard *faked his own death without telling us*, Draven. I think that ship has already flown."

"No," Draven said stubbornly. "That was different. That was Ash convincing himself that *he'd* be better off without *us*."

Silence stretched for long moments before Kade spoke again. "… Yeah. Okay, you're probably right about that " He lot out a slgh. "But I still have no clue what you think I can help you with."

"I made it worse tonight, Kade," Draven said miserably.

Kade nodded. "Sounds like you probably did, yes. The crazy idiot's been subjecting himself to rape and beatings for months now, knowing full well he could stop it at any time, but convincing himself he didn't have a choice if he wanted to get what he was after. And the worst part is, he might've succeeded and handed us that spoiled brat of a woman on a golden platter, if you hadn't gone crashing in after him. I'm guessing Ash killed the Adjunct himself, once the shit hit the turbo intake?"

The element of choice Ash must've been facing over the past weeks was an angle Draven hadn't really considered. To know that he had the option of taking out the bastard who was hurting him, and still choose every day not do it…

"He did kill Lusivian, yeah," he said absently. "I didn't even think to ask him how he managed it. He killed a bunch of guards afterward, too."

"Look, Draven," Kade said in a tired tone. "Ash might be human, but he's not a godsdamned damsel in distress. Though I expect he's carting around a freighter load of PTSD at this point, to be fair. And now you show up, all ready to claim him after years of dancing around him like a skittish *felaht*-deer? How did you *think* that was gonna go over?"

"He still needs help," Draven insisted stubbornly.

But Kade only snorted. "Oh? You think?" He shook his head, gesturing around at the freighter they were on and the empty space beyond it. "Look around us… *don't we all.* You want my advice? Try having this conversation with him when we're not up to our necks in a crisis, and keep sex the hell out of it."

"But what if we all end up dead before that happens?" Draven asked pointedly.

"Then come back in the next life and take a fresh crack at it," Kade said in a sour tone. "Maybe that life will be less fucked up than this one has been so far."

"Kade, no offense—but you realize you're really bad at this, right?" Draven said without heat.

Kade released a huff of air that in someone else might have been labeled a laugh. "Tell me something I don't know," he replied. Then he rose and crossed to Draven's chair, close enough to hook a hand around the back of Draven's neck. He gave it a small squeeze, the gesture both paternal enough and unexpected enough that it wove a thread of warmth through Draven's chest.

"Now get out of here, you damned gutter rat," Kade told him. "And for fuck's sake, go take a shower. I don't need to tell you what you smell like."

The hand slid away, and Draven vacated Kade's quarters as requested. None of what he'd just heard had been the magical answer to all his problems that he'd hoped for. Still… something Kade had said about his neurotonin addiction rattled around in Draven's head, drawing his brows together and sparking a new path through the tangled maze of his thoughts.

◆

After fleeing his cabin—and the person in it—Ash spent an unhealthy amount of time walking the freighter's corridors, barefoot and only minimally aware of his surroundings. He dimly registered that the occasional crewmembers he stumbled across were giving him some very odd looks, but it hardly mattered. Eventually, he fetched up in a massive storage bay piled high with pallets of *chik'taap* lumber.

The fragrant smell of kiln-dried wood penetrated his haze, and he blinked several times, looking around the bay. A moment later, he realized how badly he'd lost himself. He had no clue which direction he'd come in from; couldn't have described the route back to the crew quarters or the bridge from here.

Not that it was possible to become truly lost on a vessel such as this one—it was just that such lapses under other circumstances might easily become deadly. And he wasn't alone now. When he'd been with the Adjunct, it had only been his life on the line. Here, there were other people to consider. He shut his eyes, breathing in the spicy, toasted-wood scent until it chased away more of the fog shrouding his mind.

He looked down at himself. In addition to the lack of footwear, he'd been wandering around in loose nighttime clothing like a sleepwalker. Not to mention reeking of gay interspecies sex to any Vithii with a nose who got within a dozen meters of him.

Ash shut down that train of thought post-haste.

This… wasn't going to work. He needed to hold things together. He'd left someone handcuffed naked to a support strut, for fuck's sake. Not that the *someone* in question was incapable of using the key to unlock his own restraints, but—

He gave his head a sharp shake, imagining that he could hear tiny clockwork gears rattling loose inside his skull. Draven would be long gone from his quarters by now. He needed to go back and get himself sorted out. Ash might be fairly certain he was going round the bend, but he was just going to have to compartmentalize his breakdown for a little bit longer.

A quick sweep identified the nearest exit from the storage bay. Outside, a glance at a terminal readout screen next to the door showed him the layout of the ship. He trudged back to his cabin, refusing to let himself be nervous about what he might find inside when he opened it.

No surprise—it was dark and empty. He requisitioned a crew uniform in the correct size and went to take a fast shower, relieved that Kade had granted him an officer's cabin with its own small but functional lav.

The fresh clothing and boots were waiting outside his door by the time he was done. Fatigue the likes of which he'd seldom known before dragged at his body and mind. But if he hadn't been able to sleep before, he *definitely* wouldn't be able to sleep now. For a long moment, Ash wavered between going to talk with Jontalyss and going to the bridge to deal with the freighter's registration codes.

Eventually, he decided on the bridge, since he was concerned that the sharp edges grating inside his mind would prevent him from being able to have a civilized conversation with the woman. By comparison, tech was easy. He'd reprogrammed more tech while running on critical sleep deficits than he cared to remember. And while it was true that Kade's ten-cycle moratorium wasn't *quite* up yet, it was close enough that he was fairly confident the man wouldn't throw him out on his ear.

In point of fact, he wasn't even on the bridge when Ash arrived. Nor was Draven, thank all the prophets.

Ash claimed an out-of-the-way workstation and commed Kade. "It's Ash. I'm about to start work on the freighter's codes," he said, once he'd received an acknowledgement.

"*You sure you're up to it?*" Kade asked.

"Would I be here doing it if I weren't?" Ash snapped.

"*Yes*," Kade replied without hesitation.

"Your trust in me is heartwarming," Ash grated, throwing a line Kade had once fed him straight back in the Vithii's face.

"*Trust goes both ways, leetha*," Kade said. "*But don't let me keep you from what you intend to do.*"

"I'll let you know when I'm done," Ash bit off, refusing to acknowledge the sting of guilt he felt at the words. Then he flicked the switch to disconnect the call, not waiting for a reply.

The ship's computer systems were as antiquated as the rest of it, and exhaustion made the readout screens blur in Ash's vision every few minutes. He ignored that and dove into the code, pulling up the fleet database to see which of Kade's other ships would be the best candidate for registration cloning.

There was a freighter scheduled to arrive with a shipment to Terra Nova thirty-six cycles after their current estimated time of arrival. It wasn't perfect, but it was the best option of the ones he had available. He started work, switching the registration codes around at the system level and trying not to let nagging flashes of memory distract him from what he was doing.

Draven, kneeling before him… looking up the length of his body with glowing amber-gold eyes. Draven arching beneath him, a strangled cry of ecstasy tearing from his lips as he shot ropes of come over his own chest and stomach…

Ash blinked the images away angrily and focused on the numbers swimming before him. Half a cycle later, Kade came onto the bridge, and Ash finished up the final bit of code as the Vithii wandered over to him.

"All done," Ash said. "We'll scan as a freighter that was scheduled to arrive a day and a half later. You'll just have to feed them some story about scheduling conflicts or something."

Kade grunted acknowledgement. His hand fell on the back of Ash's chair, and Ash covered his involuntary flinch in reaction to the near-touch.

"If you're finished, go eat something," Kade told him. "And if you don't intend to get any more rest afterward, maybe you should go talk to your pet Regime sympathizer. We're running out of time to get her on board with the program."

Ash's jaw clenched. "Considering she's been widowed, kidnapped off-planet, physically threatened, verbally abused by complete strangers and locked in a freighter cabin, I'm not sure how you expect me to cozy up to her at this point."

Kade shrugged. "I'd be happy to snarl at her some more, *leetha*. But you seemed more interested in making nice with her—so go do that instead."

Something about Kade's continued use of the old nickname had Ash clenching the edge of the workstation until his knuckles turned white. He was appalled to realize that he wanted to whirl and shove Kade away… rail at him… curse him for daring to act like everything here was normal.

"Whatever you say," he managed, and ducked past the man he'd considered a friend and comrade for years so he could escape the bridge.

He walked fast, trying to outpace the low buzzing in his ears—like his brain was fizzing with distant static. He knew trying to deal with Jontalyss right now would be the height of foolishness, but there was no *time*. Ash came to an abrupt halt in an empty section of corridor, forcing himself to breathe until the panic subsided.

In one respect, at least, Kade had been right. Ash legitimately could not remember the last time he'd eaten, and there was little doubt that dehydration and low blood sugar were contributing to his current mental state. He took a final deep, cleansing breath and headed for whatever passed as a mess hall on this ship. He would ignore his roiling stomach long enough to eat and drink something, and then he'd tackle whatever pathetic chance was left at talking Jontalyss around to their side.

SIXTEEN

The next two days were a muddled blur of sleep interrupted by dreams, meals choked down whenever he remembered to eat, and unproductive discussions with a Vithii widow who probably still wanted Ash and everyone else on this ship dead. The only saving grace was the fact that Draven had been the picture of professionalism on those occasions when he and Ash were forced into proximity.

Mind you, that fact did nothing to stop Ash's frequent waking flashbacks about how Draven's eyes looked when he came, or the nightmares where the Adjunct's face transformed into his as Ash was choked into unconsciousness by a meaty, unrelenting hand around his throat. But things would have been far worse if Draven had gazed at him across the freighter's bridge with an expression of blame... or one of longing.

As the ship approached Terra Novan territory, Draven and Ash joined Kade on the bridge. They were still in trouble, and Ash knew it. Even with the ship masquerading as a perfectly innocent trading vessel, rather than one carrying wanted fugitives from a treaty world, they still had no good plan for what to do once they were down and docked on the surface.

The entire point of the exercise had been to talk Jontalyss around to their side so they could gain the ear of the influential Terra Novan ambassador. Since Jontalyss seemed far more likely to spit in their faces than help them, it left them at something of a loose end.

Their current less-than-compelling plan was to manufacture an engine problem that would necessitate a longer stay on the surface, in hopes that the Adjunct's widow would eventually come around. The human crewmembers might conceivably be able to apply for asylum, even if she didn't. But Ash and Draven—and by extension, Kade—were all highly sought-after criminals. If their identities were discovered, the best they could hope for would be arrest and deportation back to the Ilarian Regime, where they would face interrogation and execution.

For now, that meant they were in the familiar situation of putting one foot in front of the other, over and over, moving forward by increments despite the looming threat of disaster hanging over their heads. Ash was growing so incredibly tired of that feeling that he could weep.

"Coming within range of Terran Novan control, boss," Rita called from her station.

Kade crossed to the comm panel. He looked worn around the edges, and the paleness beneath his bronze Vithii complexion told Ash he must have dosed himself with neurotonin shortly before arriving on the bridge. It made sense, since the next few cycles would be dicey, and the last thing they needed was for him to go into withdrawal in the middle of things.

"Open a channel," Kade ordered.

The comms crackled to life, and a few moments later a female voice hailed them.

"*Ilarian freighter, your are crossing into Terra Novan controlled space. Please identify yourselves.*"

"Terra Novan control," Kade replied without hesitation. "This is interstellar freighter registration T-7256-2243-delta. Due to a scheduling conflict, we are running thirty-six cycles ahead of our previously filed ETA. Requesting permission to dock early at the New Brussels freighter port."

A pause.

"*Interstellar freighter T - 7256 - 2243 - delta, please stand by. We are scanning your ship's registration beacon for confirmation.*"

No one on the bridge looked particularly worried. Ash felt the same minor kick of adrenaline that he always felt when his coding or techworm skills faced the moment of truth, but he'd been forging ship registries for the better part of a decade now. This one would be no different than all the others.

Minutes passed, and a few of the crewmembers began to stir restlessly at their stations. Ash felt a frown pull his eyebrows together, and chided himself for succumbing to paranoia. Kade shot him an indecipherable glance from his place by the comms.

"*Ilarian freighter. Power down your main engines and maintain goosynchronous orbit using thrusters only,*" came the emotionless voice from the surface.

Kade's expression went carefully blank. He muted the comm and turned to the crewmember at the engineering console. "Do it," he said. "But keep the engines in standby mode."

Then he flicked on the comm channel. "Understood, Terra Nova. Is there a problem? We can maintain orbit until our scheduled arrival time if necessary."

This time, the reply came without a delay. *"Maintain geosynchronous orbit,"* the controller repeated. *"Your registration codes flagged the security system, and show evidence of forgery. Terra Novan defense fighters are scrambling now to your position."*

The bottom fell out of Ash's stomach as both Kade's and Draven's eyes flew to him. Neither of them looked angry. They just looked shocked, as though they couldn't even conceive of the possibility that he'd somehow made a mistake.

"Please repeat, Terra Nova?" Kade said slowly, playing for time.

Ash felt his lips part as if to say something, but his mind was flying through the process he'd used when reprogramming the ship's codes. He hadn't botched it... had he? No, he *couldn't* have. He forced himself through the memories of implementing each step—

The comms crackled. *"Repeat—your registration codes flagged the security system as showing evidence of forgery. The primary and secondary code transmissions are reading as a different registration code than the tertiary systems. Terra Novan defense fighters are scrambling to your position."*

Kade muted the channel again. "Ash?" he asked, drawing the word out.

Ash was still frozen in disbelief and denial as he obsessively ran through his actions with the codes. He thought back to the tertiary system, picturing each step, from making the new database entry, to setting up the changeover between old and new... implementing the change... confirming permissions… cross-checking… confirming the final change—

His mind drew a blank when he tried to recall hitting 'enter' on that final step. Instead, all he could picture was how tired and distracted he'd been; how ready he was to finish the job so he could go get some food, talk to Jontalyss, and try to rest again.

Nausea roiled in his gut, and he fumbled behind himself for a chair, half-falling into it.

"Oh, my gods," he breathed, as the blood drained from his face.

"That doesn't sound promising," Kade observed. "All right, then—on a scale of one to ten, how screwed are we?"

"Screwed," Ash told him, blank shock at his own mistake chasing away the horror. "We are very, *very* screwed. The tertiary systems are still transmitting the original registration code."

No one had checked his work. No one *ever* checked his work, because his work was always impeccable. *He* was the one who insisted on double-checking anything he hadn't done personally—never trusting the work of others because other people made mistakes. Other people got things wrong.

Other people. Not him.

"Brilliant," Kade muttered.

Draven looked understandably alarmed. "Wait—you mean we're still sending out the registration that has us flagged as a wanted ship? Are you *fucking serious*?"

Useless fragments of strategy whirled in Ash's mind, rendering him mute. Turn tail and flee for the nearest wormhole gate? No, the freighter was a creeping slug compared to the nimble security fighters coming after them. They couldn't run. They were unarmed; they couldn't fight. And fighting would be foolhardy anyway, when they were trying to garner allies, not more enemies—

"Draven," Kade said sharply, "take command. Stall them if you can, or just don't respond to their hails."

"Where are you going?" Ash said, barely recognizing the thready voice that emerged from his lips.

Kade shot him a dark look. "I'm going to get the spoiled brat and bring her up here to talk to them."

Ash stared back blankly. "Are you mad? She'll yell 'kidnapping and murder' before you can so much as blink!"

Draven was flicking his attention back and forth between the two of them like someone watching a hoverball match.

Kade lifted a sharp brow. "And that makes things worse how, exactly? They already know who we are. Stay here. I'll be back."

Ash watched him go, unable to formulate any additional arguments. Draven was watching him with a worried expression, but Ash couldn't formulate a response to him, either. The sick shock squeezing around his ribcage and stabbing needles through his gut was a worse feeling than being choked… a worse feeling than being whipped or punched or kicked or held down and raped.

The others had trusted him. And he'd failed them.

Ash had ensured that all of them would end up in a Regime interrogation cell, followed by an execution chamber. He'd signed his friends' death warrants. The edges of his vision went gray, and he dragged in deep breaths to keep himself from toppling into a heap on the deckplates beneath him.

"*Ilarian freighter*," came the voice from the comm. "*Defense fighters will arrive at your location in three minutes.*"

Draven squared his jaw and turned his attention from Ash to the communications board. "Terra Novan control, we're having trouble reading you. Please check the transmission channel and try again."

Kade strode back onto the bridge, dragging Jontalyss by the arm. She looked pale and rumpled, exactly like someone who'd been kidnapped from her home and dragged halfway across the Seven Systems while locked inside a tiny crew cabin. He whirled her around until she was facing him, while Draven continued to exchange transparent delay tactics with Terra Novan control in the background.

"Playtime's over now, little trophy mate," Kade growled. "We're orbiting Terra Nova, and they're about to send a bunch of fighters up here to arrest us and deport us right back to Ilarius. Now, if I'm supposed to believe your bluster, that's exactly what you want, right?"

Jontalyss glared up at him, her eyes snapping.

Kade cocked an eyebrow and continued. "I'm supposed to believe that you want to go back to your empty house... your empty *life*, where all of your dead bondmate's friends will look at you and wonder why he's in the ground and you're not. You can watch as his Regime cronies gradually shut you out of their social circles, whispering about the scandal surrounding the Adjunct's *grei'kaapt* widow and his murdering *veelaht* behind your back."

"*Fuck you*," Jontalyss snarled.

"You can watch while the internment camps are being built, and hear the news stories about human undesirables being rounded up and incarcerated," Kade continued relentlessly. "You can make bets about how long it will be before individual executions turn into mass extermination chambers, as a way to save valuable resources. Do you think the Premiere will exterminate Vithii opposition figures and humans together? Or will he make separate facilities so the two races don't have to mix while they're being gassed, or vaped into their constituent particles?"

Draven looked up from the comms, catching his eye. "Kade," he said quietly. "Time's up."

Kade gave him the barest nod of acknowledgement and turned back to Jontalyss.

"You can do all that," he said. "Or… you can talk to the nice security people here on Terra Nova, and ask to speak to your old friend, Ambassador Martinez. You can tell her what's really going on back on Ilarius, and ask her for help. You can *stand up*, for once in your damned life, and take responsibility for what's happening around you. I'll just give you a minute to decide."

Jontalyss looked like she was on the verge of tears, rage and terror chasing themselves back and forth across her lovely face. Right about now, Ash could sympathize.

Kade turned his back on her and took over the comms station from Draven.

"Terra Novan security ships, do you read?" he asked.

A new voice came across the channel—male and human. *"Ilarian freighter, this is Terra Novan security fighter alpha-one. Stand down and prepare for boarding. Any attempts to evade docking will be taken as an act of aggression."*

Ash stared at the Vithii woman trembling in the middle of the bridge, as it truly sank in that she was now their only hope for salvation. He staggered clumsily from the chair he'd fallen into, pushing past the sickening horror over his own mistake in favor of crossing to her until a bare step separated them.

She shrank back, though Ash couldn't tell if it was because she feared him or was repulsed by him. He ignored her reaction and grabbed both her hands in his, looking into her eyes. They were swimming with tears—the eyes of someone whose whole world had been reduced to a pile of rubble. The eyes of someone who had no idea what to do.

"Jontalyss," Ash pleaded. "You are all that stands between my friends and a brutal death. Once upon a time, you trusted a human and called her a friend. I'm begging you to reach out to her now and tell your friend the truth of what's happening on Ilarius. I'm *begging* you. Please help us. Don't let my friends meet the same fate my sister did."

Jontalyss' features twisted, the first tear spilling over to trail down her cheek. She jerked her hands free of his and stumbled back a step. Her eyes flitted around the bridge, taking in the mix of humans and Vithii working side by side, all of them watching the drama unfold.

Ash felt lead settle in his stomach as he stepped back and did the thing he'd bent over backward to avoid for the last decade-plus of his life—namely, acknowledging his helplessness in the situation and putting his trust in someone else to protect the people he cared for most.

Behind him, Kade was still speaking with the security squadron leader; arranging for docking and the peaceful surrender of the vessel to Terra Novan authorities. Draven's mouth was set in a grim line. Ash still felt like he might pass out.

It took less than a quarter cycle for fighters to dock at the primary and secondary docking ports. Armed Terra Novan soldiers swarmed onto the bridge, covering them as the commander strode in. Kade stepped forward, his hands raised to show he wasn't armed.

"I am Ehkadian Finisterre of Ilarius, captain of this vessel," he said. "We formally request political asylum on Terra Nova. We have among us the bondmate of a high-ranking political official. She is also a personal friend of Isadora Martinez, the Terra Novan ambassador to the planet Vithara."

The commander's cool gaze took in the bridge crew, settling on Jontalyss' tear-streaked face for a beat before returning to Kade.

"There are warrants out on this vessel and its occupants for criminal complaints on Ilarius including murder and kidnapping charges," he said. "All crew and passengers except Jontalyss Lusivian are to be arrested and held for extradition."

Ash held his breath, knowing in that moment that all was lost. This was exactly what Jontalyss would have been hoping for—the moment she could punish Ash and everyone else involved for what had happened to her. He closed his eyes.

"No," a trembling voice said. "That's not how it happened. I am Jontalyss Lusivian—that much is true. My bondmate was illegally keeping humans as slaves inside his household. *He* was the murderer. He was… a monster. He killed many such slaves in recent years. His death was not a murder. He was killed by this man in self defense."

Ash's eyes flew open to find her pointing at him. The commander's stern hazel eyes raked over him, no doubt taking in the half-healed bruises and scrapes decorating his face and neck.

Then he looked back at Jontalyss. "Are you here of your own free will, Ms. Lusivian?" he asked.

There was a beat of absolute silence. Jontalyss swallowed hard. "Yes, I—" She paused and swallowed again. "Ambassador Martinez once gave me a code to use if I ever needed to contact her for help through the Terra Novan consulate. It's secure information, but I would like to use that code now. Can I… give it to you, or…?"

The commander held her gaze evenly for a long moment, as though considering the situation.

"Come with me, ma'am," he said eventually. "There's a secure communications array inside my ship. I will connect you with the appropriate official; someone who can determine if what you say is true. In the meantime, the rest of the freighter's complement will remain here under guard."

With that, the commander escorted Jontalyss away. The other soldiers stayed behind, still covering the bridge crew. Draven let out a low whistle. Ash breathed in and out through his nose, and tried not to faint on the spot.

SEVENTEEN

More than a cycle passed before the commander returned with the Adjunct's widow. Ash couldn't read anything useful from either of their faces. A welcome numbness had woven its way through his body and mind during the long wait, making everything inside him feel as though it were wrapped in a muffling layer of gauze.

Thankfully, the Terra Novan security leader was a professional, and seemingly not prone to cruelty. He didn't leave them hanging, instead turning to address everyone present.

"The Office of Diplomatic Affairs confirms the legitimacy of Ms. Lusivian's security code. They are in the process of contacting Ambassador Martinez on Vithara via subspace communications channels. If the ambassador confirms her acquaintance with Ms. Lusivian and agrees to vouch for her, you will all be taken to the surface and your requests for asylum formally submitted for consideration."

Ash replayed the words a couple of times, but their meaning didn't change. The numbness didn't dissipate, but around him, he felt the others breathing a collective sigh of relief. Kade and Draven exchanged a guarded look with each other before their gazes landed on him, but all he could offer in response was a dazed stare.

The communications panel beeped. Rita made an abortive move to open the channel, but shrank back in her chair under the commander's stern glare. He answered it himself.

"This is Commander Jensen of Terra Novan security, in temporary command of this vessel. Request visual feed."

A few moments later, the viewscreen filled with a human face—striking, sharply cut female features topped by an elegant twist of mahogany hair.

"Commander," the woman acknowledged.

"Ambassador Martinez," the commander replied. "We have encountered a rather unusual situation. Did the Diplomatic Affairs liaison brief you?"

There was the usual lag involved in interplanetary communications before the ambassador nodded. "She did."

Commander Jensen gestured for Jontalyss to approach the comm station's video pickup. She still looked to be on the edge of tears—hugging herself tightly, with her shoulders hunched inward. She didn't say anything; just moved into the camera's range as the commander backed up a step to give her space.

The ambassador's hazel-green eyes widened, her face softening from its haughty lines even as a furrow formed between her dark brows.

"Joni?" she asked. "What's happened? My gods, are you all right?"

"*Isa*," Jontalyss choked, and burst into tears.

A suspicious tightness thickened Ash's throat, cutting through the cotton-wool feeling of nothingness. Isadora Martinez kept up a litany of soothing commentary until Jontalyss finally gained a bit of control over herself.

"That's better, sweetheart," the ambassador said. "Now tell me what's going on. What are you doing on a freighter full of fugitives in Terra Novan orbit?"

Jontalyss' expression crumpled again, but she kept herself together this time. "I need help, Isa. Everything's falling apart. There are... things happening on Ilarius. Terrible things. And I—" Her voice broke. "I was part of it. I need... *we* need political asylum. It's bad, Isa. It's really, really bad. Please help us."

Silence fell as the transmission caught up, the ambassador's expression growing grim as she listened to the words on her end. Then her expression firmed, becoming professional.

"All right, Joni," she said. "I hear you, loud and clear. Commander Jensen, I assume you're still listening. I will vouch for this asylum claim until a more in-depth investigation can be made. Please see to it that the applicants are directed to the resources they need until I can get there personally."

Lightheadedness threatened to gray out Ash's vision as their official stay of execution reached his ears.

"Very good, Ambassador," Jensen said. "I'll take care of it."

She nodded. "I was already scheduled to return to Terra Nova in three days. I'll see if I can rearrange my schedule to move that up a bit. Joni—just hang tight until we can talk in person. We'll figure this out, all right?"

"All right," Jontalyss whispered.

The ambassador gave her a strained smile, then sobered. "Keep me posted, Commander. Ambassador Martinez out."

———◆———

The Terra Novans were refreshingly efficient, it seemed. Less than a day later, the entire crew had been processed planetside. All those who desired to do so had filed official applications for asylum, pending approval by the relevant agencies.

Until everything related to the standing Ilarian request for detention and extradition was hashed out through official channels, they remained under a very liberal version of house arrest within the diplomatic housing area where the Terra Novan government was putting them up.

All of this was thanks to Ambassador Martinez, who evidently held her friendship with Jontalyss in high enough regard that she was willing to take the Vithii at her word when it came to the criminal complaints against them. It was a gilded cage, to be sure, but Ash couldn't bring himself to resent a single thing about it. Not when he'd fully expected to be imprisoned with the others for immediate trial and deportation back to their nightmare of a home planet. As it was, they'd all been assigned spacious quarters within a modern and well-appointed block of secure flats, with access to pretty much anything they needed.

Ash was… still in shock, not to put too fine a point on it.

Part of him remained half-convinced that some unseen metaphorical guillotine would descend from nowhere to chop them off at the neck, but rationality argued against that. Martinez would be on her way to speak to them personally within days, and

Jontalyss showed no inclination to change her story after finally spilling her guts to her old friend.

Ash had made no attempt to seek her out or speak with her. In fact, he'd made no attempt to seek *anyone* out and speak with them. He was still reeling from the near-disaster he'd brought down on all of their heads through the medium of his own incompetence.

In a lifetime spent careening from one crisis and disaster to another, those awful moments on the bridge of the freighter had neatly encapsulated all of Ash's worst fears, crystallizing them into a single, razor-sharp shard. That shard would remain embedded in his heart for a very long time—possibly the rest of his days. All of his silent vows that he would never, ever allow himself to be the reason any of the others died had nearly come to nothing, thanks to a single moment's inattention—a single missed keystroke on a computer terminal.

That realization had rocked Ash to his very core.

When a buzzer sounding at his door the evening after they were settled into their quarters announced Draven's arrival, Ash was not terribly surprised. He also had absolutely no idea how to deal with Draven's presence, or the topic of conversation that would no doubt ensue.

Draven gave him a single look up and down. As always, Ash got the impression that his golden eyes saw too much.

"Come with me to the common room for a bit," Draven said, easing Ash's moment of panic over the idea that a repeat of that night on the freighter might be in the offing.

"All right," Ash said, and allowed himself to be led to the tastefully appointed living area anchoring one corner of this floor of the building.

Draven sat down in one of the comfortable chairs, his Vithii frame looking ever so slightly too large for it. After a moment of hesitation, Ash perched on a chair across from him.

"I don't know where to go from here, Ash," Draven said without preamble. "When it comes to you and me, I mean. Can you help me figure it out?"

It was still mildly shocking to hear the Vithii speaking like this, even after all that had happened between them. Ash felt around for words appropriate to the situation, taking far longer to find them than he normally might.

"I'm… broken, Draven," he said when the silence threatened to grow too heavy. "I've been limping along for what seems like a very long time now, and these last couple of weeks were the last straw that finally crushed me."

"Broken things can be mended, Ash," Draven said, surprising Ash as always when he came up with some completely unexpected piece of earthy wisdom. "And sure… once something's been mended, it's not exactly the same as it was before. But maybe that's not always a bad thing, either."

Ash made himself hold that amber gaze. "I desperately want to believe you're correct about that," he said. "But I don't feel that way right now."

"So where does that leave us?" Draven asked.

"I don't know," Ash told him truthfully. "But can you accept that before I can answer that question, I need to glue a few of my pieces back together?

And I don't think that's something anyone else can help me with. Not at this point in the process."

Draven tilted his head, considering. Ash let his gaze run over those strong, familiar features, appreciating them in the new light of the Vithii's growing self-acceptance. Even as absorbed as Ash currently was in his own psychological unraveling, a part of him was pleased for Draven. After a lifetime spent hiding his true nature beneath the shadow of the intolerant culture that had reared him, his friend had finally broken free.

He was no longer allowing fear to sway his course.

"That all depends," Draven told him solemnly, "on whether you'll actually come to me when you're ready this time. Look me in the eye, and promise me on our years of friendship that you will."

A lump rose in Ash's throat, and he was appalled to feel a tightness growing in his chest—one that wanted to become the hitch of a sob. He swallowed both sensations down ruthlessly.

"I so vow," he promised. "On the strength of my regard for you, and the years of our friendship. Give me… a few days, Draven. Just let me get my feet under myself first. Then I'll come to you, and we'll talk properly."

Draven's heavy features softened into something kind and helplessly fond. "I will, Ash. When you're ready, you know where to find me."

EIGHTEEN

Draven sat at the terminal in his posh diplomatic quarters, completely failing to focus on the research he was supposed to be doing. In his defense, it was self-appointed research, and he suspected there were far more qualified people trawling through the dry text of the interplanetary agreements between Terra Nova, Vithara, and Ilarius.

Days had passed, but now that Ambassador Martinez had arrived on Terra Nova and spoken with her old college friend Jontalyss in person, things might finally start moving instead of languishing in this maddening sense of stasis. That was all for the good, since Draven didn't do well with sitting around on his ass and waiting for things to happen. He never had.

Right now, it felt like he was waiting on news from Ilarius, waiting on the Terra Novan United Council, waiting on updates from Kade about their friends, waiting on communications from Pax and Nahleene on Maelfius, waiting on…

Ash. He was waiting on *Ash*, godsdamnit.

Draven desperately wanted to ignore the human's request for time to think… time to get his shit together. He wanted to run Ash to ground in his den and fall to his knees at the human's feet, begging him to just give Draven *something*. But in addition to being humiliating, that would also be the worst thing he could possibly do, and he knew it.

After his unexpectedly frank conversation with Kade on the freighter a few days ago, Draven had visited the on-staff physician attached to the Vitharan consulate here on Terra Nova. He was sure he'd been blushing dark bronze the entire time, but he'd walked out three-quarters of a cycle later with a compact plastic case in his pocket. The case contained something that would, he hoped, make a difference when and if Ash got to the point of wanting to try moving forward with him.

It was getting late. He was still space-lagged, but maybe his concentration would improve after a night of uninterrupted sleep. With a sigh, he shut down the terminal and went to freshen up in the ridiculously ostentatious lav attached to the suite. Seriously, the humans on Terra Nova seemed almost obsessive about their giant bathtubs and extravagant shower stalls. Maybe it was just the difference between living on a planet that was swimming with fresh water, versus one like Ilarius where water resources had to be carefully managed to prevent shortages.

Draven showered and dried off with a fluffy towel pulled from a *heated towel rack*, of all the fucking things. He couldn't help snorting in jaded amusement at the idea of a gangland gutter rat from the Capital undercity staying in a place like this—acting like some high-and-mighty diplomatic envoy.

The whole situation was completely and utterly *whacked*.

A buzzer sounded at the entrance to his quarters, muted by the bathroom door and the towel over his head as he scrubbed at his spiky, copper-colored hair. He frowned, but there were no crises looming here; no reason to think he or anyone else was in danger.

"Just a minute!" he called, tossing the towel aside and grabbing his trousers.

It was probably Kade, even though a corner of his mind hoped for someone else. He dragged on the trousers and fastened them, padding barefoot to the door to see what the older Vithii wanted.

"Sorry about that," he said, as the door slid open. "I was just—"

The words trailed off, his heart stuttering once before settling into a faster rhythm.

"Hello, Draven," Ash said.

The human stood in the corridor, looking wan but composed. For the first time in far too long, his face and neck were free of bruises and scrapes, and his eyes, while tired, no longer radiated unspoken pain. He was dressed formally in a tailored charcoal suit with the triangular chest flap buttoned in place across the front, as though he'd just come from an important meeting or something. And who knows—maybe he had.

His black hair was pulled back and tied into a tight queue at the nape of his neck. Draven couldn't stop staring at him; drinking him in.

A faint smile tugged at one corner of the human's lips, though his expression still held a lost air. "Care to invite me inside?" he prompted, breaking Draven out of his momentary trance.

He twitched in place, and blinked twice. "Uh… come in?"

Ash's features softened, his smile growing a bit less wistful a moment before it faded. "Love to," he said, brushing past Draven like a whisper and looking around the room as though it were something fascinating.

Draven tried to remember how civilized people acted when in civilized surroundings. "Um, sit down wherever, I guess. You want a drink or anything?"

"Gin, if you have it," Ash replied, unbuttoning the flap of his lapel and letting it hang free, revealing a triangle of crisp white shirt beneath.

Draven caught himself staring again and dragged his eyes away in favor of crossing to the minibar. When he emerged a few moments later with the bottle of gin in hand, it was to find Ash seated at the small breakfast table next to the floor-to-ceiling windows set in the far wall. He juggled the bottle in one hand and two cut-glass tumblers in the other, setting everything down and pouring each of them a generous measure.

Then he sat across from Ash and took a steadying drink, ignoring the fact that human gin was completely disgusting stuff. Ash lifted his glass as well, sipping at the contents and watching Draven's face with a single-mindedness that was more than a little disconcerting. Draven glanced at the window next to him to escape the weight of that gaze, but the lighting inside the suite overpowered all but the brightest of the lights from the human city beyond—turning the glass into more of a mirror than a portal to the outside world.

"I still don't know exactly what you want from me, Draven," Ash said at length, nothing angry or accusatory in his tone—only tired.

Draven's eyes snapped back to him. "I don't want anything from you," he replied, realizing too late that the words had come out sounding all wrong.

But Ash only gave him a flicker of that exhausted half-smile again, and shook his head. "Yes, you do."

Draven swallowed and tried to collect his thoughts. "Okay. Yes. You're right. I want... us to be together. I want to protect you."

The human continued to watch him intently as he spoke. "We're at the epicenter of a civil war. You can't protect me from that—any more than I was able to protect you, back on Ilarius. But right now, we're both sitting safe and comfortable on a neutral planet. So I don't need protecting."

Draven stared back at him. "I think you do, though." He shook his head, frustrated. "But I'm not saying it right. I... want to be your haven. I want to be the one you come to, like Skye goes to Hunter, or Temple goes to Ryder."

Ash swirled his gin, looking down at it. "A haven? Hmm. I don't think I've ever had one of those."

Draven screwed up his courage, reaching across the small table to cover Ash's free hand lightly with his. "Yes, you have," he said. "You've just always refused to use it."

A small noise caught in Ash's throat—so soft that a human probably wouldn't have been able to hear it. But Draven did.

"Ash," he said quietly.

The human was silent for several seconds before speaking.

"I still haven't contacted my parents to inform them I'm here on Terra Nova," he said, in an apparent non sequitur.

"Why not?" Draven asked after a slight pause, not letting go of Ash's hand.

Ash turned to stare at the window as though he could see past the reflection of his own face, to the city beyond. "I had a sister. Did you know that?"

"You mentioned her, when you were talking to Jontalyss on the freighter," Draven said. "She died, I'm guessing?"

Ash nodded, still not looking at him. "She made the mistake of speaking out publicly against Kovak when he was still a Minister, before he became the Premiere. And then *I* made the mistake of trusting my parents when they said not to worry—that they'd taken care of her security."

"Kovak had her killed?"

Ash shrugged a shoulder. "Presumably. She died in mysterious circumstances, and the official investigation into her death was stonewalled from the beginning."

Draven let out a breath. "That was when you got your parents off-planet?

Dark eyes sought his, and held. "Yes. But more importantly, it was when I learned that I couldn't rely on other people to take care of the things that are most important to me," he said. "Not even the people whom I should be able to trust."

Draven let that sink in for a few moments, rolling it around in his head to extract the nuances. "Explains quite a bit about you, I guess," he said at length.

"Does it?" The human's brows drew together, and relaxed an instant later. "Maybe it does."

Draven nodded. "You've been trying to take every godsdamned thing on your own shoulders, barreling headfirst toward the day when it would all be too much, and end up exploding in your stupid face."

Ash paled visibly beneath his dusky olive complexion. "That day very nearly occurred on the freighter."

"Yes, it did," Draven agreed. "But it worked out okay, all things considered."

Silence settled over them, heavy and deep.

"I want—" Ash began, only to cut himself off.

"What do you want?"

"So many things," the human said on a sigh. "If I'm going to go charging back into civil war and genocide, I want to remember what it feels like to truly trust again… before I have to give my life for a cause, or watch other people I care about give their lives. But I'm afraid."

Draven thought he understood. "You're worried it will affect your judgment."

"Something like that."

He thought for a moment, trying to decide how best to make the words come out so he wouldn't make a hash of things again. While he was doing that, Draven slid his hand back a few centimeters and splayed his fingers, inviting Ash to interweave their hands together. After a pregnant pause, Ash did, twining their fingers and squeezing convulsively.

And for the first time since the human had walked through the door, Draven thought that maybe—*just maybe*—this could finally, actually work.

"Ash," he said, "your judgment when it comes to the rest of us is already shit. That's not gonna change if you let me take care of you and make you feel good. You *staged your own death* to try to protect us, never realizing that was the quickest way to make me come running after you. Admitting that you need this as much as I do won't make you any stupider about protecting us than you already are right now."

Ash released a sharp breath that was probably a laugh—though there was a sense behind it of something stretched to the breaking point.

"Bloody hell, Draven," he murmured. "Do you have to be so *painfully* right about things?"

Draven squeezed his hand briefly. "Hey, now… I could get used to hearing you say I'm right about stuff. Someone better make a note of the date and time."

Ash's laugh this time was low, but genuine. "You'd grow bored of me in no time if I turned into a sycophant." He sobered, a furrow marring his brow. "I've been playing that role for too long as it is."

Draven nodded. "You're right. That's not what I want from you. I just want the truth. I want to know what you need—because it sure as hell wasn't what happened in your quarters on the freighter a few nights ago."

"No." The word was faint, and Ash slowly withdrew his hand from Draven's. He straightened his shoulders as though steeling himself. "That's the thing. I don't know if I can give you what *you* need, even though not so long ago, I would have wanted it just as much."

"You mean sex," Draven said bluntly.

"Yes."

"I've been thinking about that. You know they make those, whaddya call them—*sleeves*, right?" Draven asked.

Ash blinked at him.

Draven shrugged. "I'm just saying. If we were doing… something else, and I shot my load unexpectedly, like I did that first time, then *boom*. I could just grab the sleeve and stick my dick in it. I guess you can get ones that are heated to Vithii body temperature, and supposedly they feel a lot like being inside someone. As long as I could hold you in my arms while I was knotting it, things wouldn't be so bad."

The series of expressions that chased themselves across Ash's features came and went too fast for Draven to keep up, so he forged ahead.

"But I don't know if you can get those here, so in the meantime, I picked up a couple of hypos from a Vitharan doctor at the consulate," he said.

Ash's features settled into a look of confusion. "Hypos? What for?"

"Yeah, hypos. They're loaded with a pre-measured dose of fast-acting sedative calculated for my bodyweight," Draven explained. "Though the sedative action's more of a side effect, in this case. The important thing is, the stuff'll deflate my knot within seconds. Of course, I'd also be really out of it for half a cycle or so, but I thought maybe that could be useful, too? Like, you could hold onto one of them, and if things ever got too intense or you started having a flashback, you could jab me with it. Then I'd be helpless and you'd know you were safe."

Something Draven couldn't identify flashed in Ash's eyes, and the human looked away quickly, raising a hand to his temple to block Draven's view of his expression. Draven's stomach dipped when he saw that Ash's shoulders were shaking silently.

"Ash?" he asked. "What is it? I'm sorry... I didn't mean—"

"No, stop," Ash rasped, and his hand shot out to capture Draven's again. The human took a steadying breath. "You just… have to keep upending my expectations, don't you?"

Draven's brows drew together. "I don't know what you mean."

Ash looked at him, eyes bright with unshed tears—helplessly fond. "I know you don't. That's the part that's killing me."

Then, before Draven realized what he was doing, Ash lifted Draven's hand and brought his wrist to his mouth, leaning forward to close lips and teeth over the tendon. Draven's pulse jumped, and he drew in a sharp breath as Ash sucked a Vitharan love bite into his skin, giving the bruise a final sharp nip before lowering his arm back to the table.

NINETEEN

Draven stared at his wrist like it belonged to someone else, unable to look away from the small red mark. When that didn't do anything to kick his brain into gear, he looked up at Ash instead. The human smiled, but his eyes still held that sheen of tears, covering a look of sadness and worry.

"I have a proposal for you," Ash said. "One on which I very well may be unable to follow through. Would you like to hear it?"

"Yes," Draven said blankly.

Ash nodded, as though to himself. "I wasn't lying when I told you I wasn't a top, and have no desire to become a top."

Draven nodded back, still struck dumb.

"You've bent over backward to try to reassure me about my safety when I'm with you," Ash continued. "And… well, the truth is—it's not that simple. It's not just that I panic. Sometimes I dissociate completely. The last few times Denrir took me, my mind shut down as soon as he entered me. The gods only know how much important intel I may have missed when he was flapping his lips in the afterglow."

Rage wasn't helpful now, even if Draven wanted to hire a ship and fly back to Ilarius just so he could unearth the Adjunct's bloated corpse from its grave and rip its limbs off. He had to keep reminding himself that Ash didn't need rescuing. Hell, Ash had been the one *doing* the rescuing—killing the Adjunct and the guards to get Draven free. Draven closed his eyes and breathed slowly through his nose until the red haze across his mind lifted.

"Okay," he said, instead of any of the stupid territorial shit that wanted to fly out of his mouth. "Do you think there's anything we could do that would help with that?"

Ash paused. "I don't know for certain… but I'm willing to try. As long as you understand that there's a chance I might—" He broke off and swallowed audibly. "Harm you… or try to, anyway. If I forget that you're you, and not someone else, I mean."

Draven nodded. "That's all right. I'll even give you the right weapon to use—the hypo. You can poke me with it the instant you need to, and all it will do is put me to sleep for a bit."

Ash pushed his chair back and rose, crossing to Draven's side of the table. Draven pushed his chair back as well, but Ash placed a light hand on his shoulder, keeping him from rising. A moment later, Draven had a lapful of warm human male as Ash straddled him. His dick surged to full awareness, straining against his trousers.

And Ash… kissed him. He recognized the human gesture for what it was immediately, even if his body didn't quite know what to do with it.

His mind did, though. This was an act that no perverted Vithii filth would ever have conceived of doing to a *veelaht*. It was untainted—something just for them. He was afraid to take the human in his arms; afraid it would feel too much like restraint, with the sedative hypos nowhere in sight. So he contented himself with cupping one hand around

Ash's elbow, not gripping… and let the human teach him how to kiss.

Draven knew his lips were rough and chapped, but he could feel them growing warm and slick beneath the velvet slide of mouth on mouth. Ash tasted like mint, and the gin he'd sipped from the glass Draven had poured for him. He kissed with his whole body, as though Draven was the center of his universe and nothing else existed beyond the two of them.

As though he never wanted to stop.

Unsure of himself—but desperate to make certain that Ash got every single thing he needed tonight—Draven carefully tried to mirror what the human was doing, making mental notes of what actions drew the most positive responses. Small noises, muffled by the press of Draven's lips. A shiver. A flex of the hips.

Without Draven intending it, their cocks brushed through two layers of clothing, drawing a low rumble from his chest. Ash broke away from the kiss and drew in a sharp breath—stiffening… but not fleeing, thank the gods.

"It's all right," Draven said quickly. "You're all right. It's just me—nothing's gonna happen that you don't want. Here, let me up and we'll go get the hypo so you can have it handy."

Ash dipped his head, a snort of rueful laughter escaping. "*Breathe*, Draven. I'm not quite that much of a mental case yet. Sorry. It's fine. Just… not used to things feeling… *good*… like this. It's been a while, to say the least."

Draven nudged him upright anyway. Ash backed up a step and leaned hipshot against the edge of the table, looking down at him.

"I still want you to have it before we go much further," Draven said.

"All right. If it will make you feel better," Ash agreed.

"And I want you to tell me everything you can think of that you *don't* want me to do to you," he continued.

The human looked away, his eyes growing distant.

"I know it's a mood-kill," Draven told him. "But I need to know. And you only have to do it once, unless you think of something else to add later."

Ash huffed, somewhere between amused and irritated. "Playing psychologist now? And here I thought I'd be stuck footing the bill for expensive therapy sessions at some point in the future... if I lived that long."

"*Pfft*. You know Ryder would give you a discount if you asked."

A look of genuine horror crossed Ash's face. "*Ryder*? Oh, *gods*, no."

Draven shrugged. "Fortunately for you, talking to her is optional. Talking to *me* isn't."

Ash pushed away from the table and began to wander aimlessly around the room. Draven knew very well about needing to move so you didn't crawl out of your own skin, and let him be while he collected his thoughts.

"All right, then. You asked for it," the human said eventually. "Don't order me to strip. Or to undress you."

"I'm not gonna order you to do anything," Draven tried to reassure him.

But Ash only shot him a look of jaded amusement. "You just ordered me to talk to you, not thirty seconds ago," he pointed out mildly.

Draven opened his mouth... and closed it again. "Yeah. I guess I did at that. But... go on. I'm still listening."

The human's smile grew more genuine before he sobered again. "I know you are." He continued to pace slowly around the room, one of his hands rising to brush absently at his neck, where the slave collar would have rested. "Don't grab or pull my hair," he said in a distant tone. "Don't put your hands or anything else around my throat. Don't cut off my airways, or break my skin. In fact, don't leave marks on me at all."

Draven's throat threatened to close up as he realized that these things had clearly happened to Ash at the Adjunct's hands. But all he said was, "I won't."

Ash fetched up against the doorframe of the room's entrance and let out a bitter rasp of a laugh. "You'd never guess it now, but I used to enjoy a bit of pain with my pleasure. Bondage Boy—that was me. It's what made me think I might be able to pull off this *veelaht* act in the first place." He shook his head sharply, as if in disgust. "And you were right, by the way—this *is* a total mood-kill."

"Yeah, it is," Draven agreed. "But it's better than the alternative of stumbling over a landmine with no warning. And anyway, it's done now."

"I suppose."

"It is," Draven insisted. "So tell me now about things you enjoyed, from... before. Not the kinky shit, though. Nothing that's been ruined for you— just things that you used to do, and liked."

Ash appeared to think about the question for some considerable time.

"Kissing," he said, at length. "Kissing for ages, the way teenagers do. Fellatio. Giving and receiving… though I can't promise anything on the giving front, right now."

"Told you already," Draven reminded him. "I'm not all that interested anyway. Though if you change your mind, we can try playing around with it, I guess. Go on."

"Being opened up. *Slowly*," Ash said. "Being teased open as though the teasing is the whole point, rather than something to get out of the way so your partner can fuck you."

Draven nodded slowly, even though Ash's gaze was distant, not looking at him. "Those sound like good things," he said. "I want you to have those things again, Ash. I want *us* to have them."

And now Ash's gaze locked with his, dark and sad and maybe—just *maybe*—a little bit hopeful.

"Will you show me more about human kissing now?" Draven asked. "I want to learn. I want to learn all of it—everything that you like, even if it doesn't all have to happen tonight."

Ash watched him for a moment that seemed to stretch between them. "Yes," he said. "But not here. Take me to bed, please."

Draven rose, feeling warmth spread through him like sunlight breaking through the clouds of an endless winter. His heart beat strong and steady in his chest as his instincts to protect and care for this prickly, stubborn human rose within him like an inexorable tide. This was what they had both needed for so long, and now… *finally*… it seemed their time had come.

He led Ash into the suite's airy bedroom, with its tasteful fixtures and sprawling bed. When they were both inside, Draven turned and closed the small amount of distance between them, trying to recreate Ash's kiss from earlier, only in reverse. Maybe he was starting to get the hang of it after all, because the human yielded beneath his lips and tongue—pliant and giving.

They kissed until Draven was lightheaded before reluctantly parting for air. He straightened, putting enough space between them that he could finger the lapel of Ash's suit jacket.

"Can I take this off?" he asked.

"Yes," Ash murmured. "Take all of it off, if you like. It's fine."

Draven kissed him again, and then started working on buttons and fasteners. The jacket went easily enough, but the crisp white shirt beneath was fiddly, with tiny buttons spaced all down the front. Ash helped him by undoing the cuffs while he was working his way down the human's chest and stomach. Finally, he tugged the shirttails free of Ash's trousers and pushed the shirt off Ash's shoulders... only to reveal a white cotton undershirt beneath.

"Too many layers," he complained.

Ash gave a breathless little laugh. "Should I have shown up in a one-piece Velcro jumpsuit? Or a bathrobe? Don't begrudge me this opportunity to wear a damned suit, you hulking Vithii Luddite."

Draven helped him pull the undershirt off. "Oh, don't get me wrong. I thoroughly approve of the suit. It's just a fucking pain to get you out of it, that's all. Will you take your hair out of the tie? I promise I won't touch it."

Ash raised his eyebrows. "I… can do that, yes. But you're lucky, you know—I came very close to hacking all of it off while we were on the freighter."

Draven paused. "It wouldn't have mattered if you had. But I do like the way it looks when it's long."

Ash reached for the binding tying the thick braid into a neat, club-shaped queue and started untying it. "In the end, cutting it off seemed a bit too much like running up the white flag," he said absently. "So the hair got a stay of execution—for now, at least. I'll probably regret it the next time I get dragged into hand-to-hand combat."

Draven ruffled his own short spikes. "I'd say, 'then don't get dragged into hand-to-hand combat,' but…"

The look Ash shot him was rueful. "Quite so."

Black hair fell loose over Ash's shoulders, and Draven took a selfish moment to appreciate the picture he made—naked from the waste up, with his sensual lips shiny and swollen from kissing. Then he shook himself free of his preoccupation and went into the lav, where the plastic case containing the pre-loaded hypos lay nestled in a drawer.

He took one out. While he was at it, he also grabbed a little tub of petroleum jelly that he'd noticed earlier in the mirrored cabinet above the sink, in case it ended up being useful at some point. Returning to the bedroom, he discovered that Ash had continued without him, slipping off his shoes, socks, and trousers. The human now sat on the edge of Draven's bed with one knee drawn up and his forearm resting across it, wearing only a pair of black boxers.

"Here," Draven said, shamelessly drinking in the sight. He proffered the little hypo cylinder. "You should take this now. It's an auto-injector, so you just need to make sure it's pointing the right way around and jam it into me wherever you can reach."

Ash took it, setting it aside on the bed with a nod and a sad smile. "I'll keep it in mind."

Next, Draven lifted the tub of petroleum jelly so Ash could see it. "Is this, um… all right to use? If you still want to… do that later, I mean."

"It's fine for tonight," Ash said. "Now come kiss me some more. You're hovering, and it's making me jumpy."

Draven huffed, but didn't argue. Ash crab-crawled backward until he was fully on the bed, and Draven followed him, stalking forward on hands and knees. After a moment's consideration, he settled himself next to Ash rather than looming over him. He also grabbed the abandoned hypo from the foot of the bed and plopped it down within easy reach of Ash's right hand.

Then Ash was hooking his fingers around the back of Draven's neck and pulling him down until their lips met once more, stealing his breath and his focus until all he could think about was the feeling of mouth on mouth and skin on skin. Draven loved the fact that he could tell the whole time whether Ash was okay, based on the fact that was still holding Draven in place and ravishing him with lips and tongue.

When the human's movements grew slow and drugged, Draven gave into the urge to taste more of him. "No marks," he promised, and started making his way lower.

For now, he passed over the tempting column of Ash's throat, worried that it might be too much. Instead, he ran his lips over the jut of a collarbone, careful not to succumb to his natural desire to bite. Ash's hand remained a heavy, encouraging weight at the nape of his neck.

When Draven flicked his tongue curiously over the pebbled brown point of Ash's nipple, the human shuddered. The tent he was pitching in his loose boxers argued that it had been a good kind of shudder, so Draven did it again. Then he repeated the action on the other nipple, to compare the results. Ash let out a strangled noise, his hand tightening.

"Yes, all right, damn you—you've found a weakness I neglected to mention," he said breathlessly. "But I'll remind you that even good torture *is still torture.*"

Draven huffed a breath of amusement across the taut nub of flesh, and Ash's hips flexed off the bed. He could have happily taken longer with what he was doing, but he could also recognize a hint when he saw one. So he straightened away from Ash's guiding hand on his nape, in favor of hooking his fingers into the waistband of the black boxers and sliding them off.

The human was still breathing deeply, not showing any sign of distress at being unclothed, so Draven dropped his head and wrapped his lips around Ash's jutting erection, sliding down to take as much of it into his mouth as he could.

"*Bloody... buggering...*" Ash panted. His hips jerked up, and Draven followed the movement to keep from choking. "I still can't... wrap my brain around the idea of you being a… closeted *cock slut* all this time…"

Draven backed off, letting Ash's dick slide out of his mouth with a wet pop. "I was a closeted *everything*, wasn't I? What makes this any different? Besides, you taste good."

He expected some kind of witty comeback. But apparently—after all these years—he'd finally discovered the key to shutting Ash up.

"I want to open you up now," Draven said. "You can reach my shoulder with the hypo if you need to, right?"

Ash stayed silent and still for a moment before blowing out a slow breath. "Let me worry about that part, you great menace. Just… take your time with it, please. I'm still self-flagellating for making your first experience with penetration what it was."

Draven shot him a look that was half-exasperated, half-sheepish. "I came like a damned blast cannon afterward, didn't I?" he asked pointedly.

The human sighed. "Which still doesn't mean I was right to treat you that way."

Draven blinked at him. "You know what? I think I liked it better when you were speechless," he decided, and swallowed Ash's cock again.

TWENTY

Ash felt another choked noise escape his control, and he let his head drop back to rest on the mattress as he tried to remember what it was like to be pleasured for pleasure's sake.

Prophets.

Draven might have been unpracticed at both sex and seduction, but he was a godsdamned natural at it. It was a bloody *crime* that the world had been deprived of his care and enthusiasm for loving another man before now.

The hypo of sedative lay a few inches from his right hand, where Draven had set it earlier—but Ash refused to clutch the blasted thing like a security blanket. For now, he was all right. It was possible that would change once Draven got a finger inside him—but this was such a different scenario than the brutal assaults that had fractured his psyche, Ash felt he ought to be able to keep the two things separate.

In fact, he was starting to wonder if his bitter assertion on the freighter—that he wouldn't be able to come from Draven's mouth on him—had been a lie. Maybe his sexual response wasn't quite as broken as it had seemed these past months, because the heat coiling at the base of his spine wasn't bringing along the associated panic this time.

Draven pulled away from Ash's cock again, giving him a few moments of respite. The pop of

the jar lid opening had no negative associations—
Denrir never used lube beyond his own naturally
occurring slick. Nor did the gentle manhandling as
Draven moved Ash's legs apart so he could settle
between them. Denrir would have slit his own wrists
before voluntarily getting his face anywhere near
Ash's cock.

Even so, Ash's body jolted at the first brush of
fingers along his crease. Draven stilled immediately.

"No?" the Vithii asked cautiously.

Ash willed his muscles to unclench, one by
one. "*Yes*. Just… give me a minute."

The fingers drew away. "I could go back to
sucking you instead," Draven suggested.

Ash swallowed to moisten his throat. "Counter-
proposal for you. How are you at multitasking?"

Draven snorted. "Since I've got no idea what
I'm doing down here, I probably won't be any worse
at doing two things at once than I would be doing
one at a time."

Wet heat enclosed the head of his cock before
Ash could reply, a raspy tongue curling around the
glans in a sinuous curve.

"That's the spirit," he managed.

This time, when the slick fingers brushed over
his hole, he focused instead on the sensations in
his cock. But Draven had apparently taken his mention of slow teasing to heart, and appeared to be in
no hurry. Rather than pressing inside immediately,
he continued to massage the edges of Ash's opening with slow circles. A lovely, melting feeling that
he hadn't experienced in far too long spread outward from the two points of contact, and Ash let out
a stuttering breath.

Draven must have felt him relax into the dual sensations, because he hummed in satisfaction. Slowly, Ash settled into the headspace of trusting what was being done to him—releasing the tight guard he'd held around himself for so many long, terrible weeks. By the time Draven finally got around to breaching him, the combination of relaxation and the amount of hard use his arse had seen recently meant that his thick finger slid inside easily.

And… it was good. It felt like being filled up; not like being assaulted. Draven—bless him—had no clue about finding the human prostate. That suited Ash perfectly right now. Forced orgasm might be a staple in the pornography industry, but it was also a real thing—and there was absolutely nothing sexy about it. At this point, Ash was very much afraid that prostate orgasms had been forever ruined for him. And honestly, he wasn't quite ready to have that theory confirmed.

Soon, perhaps… but not yet.

For now, being on the receiving end of a delightfully unpracticed blowjob while Draven patiently stroked him open was all kinds of bliss. When a third blunt finger joined the two already scissoring inside him, the pleasurable pressure surged, tightening his balls.

"*Draven*," he choked, "I—"

Draven made a spirited attempt to swallow his prick whole, and Ash arched off the bed helplessly as his release crashed over him, startling in its intensity. When he could make sense of his surroundings again, Draven had pulled off his dick and slid his fingers out of Ash's arse. He had a little smear of Ash's semen dribbling down his chin, and they were both breathing hard.

"Come up here," Ash managed, guiding Draven up the length of his body with clumsy hands.

Draven frowned. "Do you really want me to kiss you right after I—"

Ash cut off the question by dragging him down until their lips crashed together, licking into his mouth to chase his own taste. Draven made a startled noise into the kiss, and cursed in Vithii when Ash moved lower to lap the spilled drops off his chin.

They rested together for a few moments, forehead to forehead. Draven had evidently been rendered speechless, and Ash felt like someone had turned his body into melted toffee. It would have been exceptionally easy to bask in the afterglow of the shattering orgasm until it faded and his brain started working again. But the easy way had never worked for the two of them.

"Trousers off," Ash ordered. "We're doing this now, while my brain is still a puddle of goo."

To his credit, Draven didn't ask if he was sure about his decision. Ash was *never* going to be sure, so such a question would only have been irritating. Instead, Draven kissed him again, brief and fierce.

"All right. It's your choice. How do you want me?" he asked.

Ash wasn't really up to devising strategy right now, even for something as simple as getting fucked. But he did his best to cast his mind back to *before*… to the things he'd enjoyed in the time where he wasn't a shattered mess.

"Grab the pillows and prop yourself up against the headboard," he said. "I'm about to introduce you to the human concept of *reverse cowboy*."

At which point I may or may not freak out on you, he didn't add… since Draven was already well aware of the possibility.

Draven rolled off the bed and grabbed a steri-wipe for his greasy hand before working on the fastenings of his trousers. He wasn't wearing anything underneath, and Ash forced himself to watch—poking at his own emotional reaction to seeing the restlessly flexing python of a cock that the Vithii had been hiding beneath the fabric.

"Do humans give all of their sex positions ridiculous names?" Draven asked quizzically.

"Oh, yes," Ash said, glad of the distraction from the unwanted flutter of panic teasing the edges of his awareness. "*Invariably*. Ask me sometime about the butter churner, or the standing wheelbarrow."

Draven shot him a look. "Your species is very strange. You realize that, right?"

"You don't know the half of it," Ash agreed, trying to ignore the clammy sweat breaking out on his body as Draven positioned himself at the head of the bed, sitting with his muscular legs stretched out in front of him.

"All right," Draven said. "I'm dribbling so much slick for you that it's getting embarrassing, you crazy bastard. Now pick up that damned hypo, will you? Because this isn't happening unless you're holding onto it and ready to use it."

Breathing deeply in an attempt to keep his mind centered, Ash reluctantly picked up the hypo. He didn't want to use it. He didn't want to *need* it. He wanted to erase the last few months completely, and go back to a time when he could have enjoyed every moment of this new and wonderful thing that was about to happen between them. It irked him terribly that Draven should be thrust into the role of caretaker like this, when it should be *Ash* reassuring *him* about what they were doing together.

But none of that was helpful right now. Ash was the one likely to lose his shit, and Draven was giving every indication that he had, in fact, finally come to terms with his own desire for other males. If Ash's staged death and the subsequent clusterfuck at the Adjunct's residence had been responsible for that change, then perhaps something good had come out of it in the end.

But now he was just stalling.

He shook his head at himself, hating the feeling of his heart racing inside his chest. Once upon a time, he'd been good at this... good at being a lover, good at pleasing a willing partner. Now, it was all he could do to straddle Draven's lap, his back to Draven's front, the hypo clutched in his right hand.

"Ash..." Draven said, sounding uncertain.

"No. Just let me do this," Ash said hoarsely.

Draven shuddered beneath him as Ash rubbed against the flexing, seeking cock nestled between his arse cheeks. Without either warning or finesse, he changed the angle until the blunt tip was positioned at his entrance.

The man beneath him might have been inexperienced, but Vithii cocks generally knew exactly what they wanted, and this one wanted to be inside of Ash. Draven hadn't been joking about the amount of slick he was pumping out, either—the stretch and burn of penetration would probably have been minimal if Ash weren't so tense.

"*Gods*," Draven breathed.

A large hand cupped his left shoulder, and Ash twitched uncontrollably even though there was nothing threatening or confining about the touch.

"I'm all right," he said quickly, even though Draven hadn't asked. Ash could hear desperation threading through his tone, and he hated it.

Draven's voice sounded strained, but sincere when he said, "Ash. We don't have to do this tonight. Or *ever*. You know that, right?"

But I do, Ash thought. *I have to know if I still can.*

Aloud, he only said, "It's fine."

And then, he started to move. In this position, he couldn't see Draven's expression, and that was good. Even better, Draven couldn't see *his* expression. When Denrir wasn't taking Ash on his hands and knees like an animal, the Adjunct had often pinned him on his back by his throat, so he could stare fixedly at Ash's face while offering a running commentary of humiliating observations.

Ash moved up and down mechanically, all his focus devoted to shutting out the past. Draven was holding himself still except for the occasional tremor and the restless, involuntary twisting of his cock. But he was also a virgin, or damned close to it, and it wasn't long before his muscles grew tense beneath Ash's steady rise and fall.

"Ash," he warned. "I think… I'm getting close. Need you to… talk to me, yeah? We can still stop—
"

"We're not stopping," Ash grated, the words far too harsh for the situation. He tried to ignore the nauseated feeling churning in his gut as he moved faster, while attempting to keep the cock in his arse angled away from his prostate as much as possible.

Draven choked on a curse and convulsed beneath him, spilling inside Ash with a series of twitching spurts. Ash stilled, shaking… frozen between his determination to see this through even if it killed him, and the panicked desire to drag himself off Draven's cock while he still could, before fleeing the room entirely.

But then it was too late. Draven's knot swelled, trapping them together and pressing against the most vulnerable places inside him—inexorable and inescapable. Ash's body jerked, going rigid even as his ragged breathing accelerated and a gray haze closed in around the edges of his vision. Awareness of his surroundings faded away, replaced by horrors from the recent past.

"*Ash,*" a voice said sharply, sounding as though it were coming through a staticky long-range comm system.

Ash opened his mouth, fully intending to reply—but all that came out was a strangled whimper.

TWENTY-ONE

Draven felt Ash's body going rigid, his breathing becoming fast and uneven.

"*Ash*," he said sharply, fighting the post-orgasmic haze blanketing his mind as his knot swelled, locking the two of them together.

The human's only response was a pained, almost animalistic noise of fear that made dread pool in his stomach. Not sure if it would help or make things even worse, Draven wrapped an arm around him to ensure he didn't try to lunge away and tear himself all to hell in the attempt.

"Ash?" he repeated. "I need you to talk to me. Don't check out on me now, okay? You can use the hypo if you need to…"

There was no reply except the sound of Ash's spirited attempts to hyperventilate. Draven tried not to panic right along with him; instead, he ran his free hand down to cover Ash's. The human was still holding the hypo in nerveless fingers, so Draven guided it around until the business end was resting against his hip, ready to be used.

"I swear to all the gods and prophets, Ash—if you don't answer me in the next ten seconds, I'll do this myself," he warned.

His head was swimming with the need to protect and comfort, but he made himself count down the seconds while his other hand rubbed slow circles over Ash's sternum.

"C'mon, Ash," he urged. "Or I'm stopping this whole thing in five… four… three… two…"

Ash made an anguished noise and jerked the hypo out of Draven's loose grip, throwing it across the room with startling violence.

"I hate this," the human gasped. "I *hate* it. I hate what I let that vicious bastard do to me—"

Draven swallowed a curse as the hypo clattered against the wall, hopelessly out of reach. For lack of any better idea, he wrapped his other arm around Ash as well, holding him as the human shook apart before his eyes.

"Breathe," he said. "Ash, just breathe with me for a minute, okay? I've got you; I swear I won't let anything bad happen. Just stay with me. One breath at a time."

He made himself breath slowly and evenly, even though his body was awash with mating instincts—a chemical cocktail of hormones. Ash's heart thudded against his palm, pounding against its cage of flesh and bone. But after a few more awful seconds, he drew in a breath and held it, only letting it shudder free of his lungs when Draven breathed out against his back.

The next breath was a painful gasp, and so was the one after that, but his chest rose and fell in time with Draven's. Draven closed his eyes in relief, maintaining the slow rhythm in and out, until the racing heartbeat beneath his hand started to slow.

"Tell me what you need," he tried, but Ash could only shake his head.

So Draven went back to what he'd been doing before—breathing in, holding it for a few seconds, breathing out. He once again started rubbing steady circles over the smooth skin beneath his palm. They stayed that way for long minutes, while Draven tried to somehow will his knot to go away.

Unfortunately, Vithii biology didn't work that way.

The human in his arms was a bundle of tense muscles and nerves, shuddering every few seconds as his body and mind fought each other for control. Not sure what else to do, Draven started murmuring soothing nonsense, repeating over and over that he was here, that Ash was safe. Gradually, the violent tremors grew further apart and of shorter duration. As time passed, that horrible rigidity began to fade, and Ash sagged against him by increments.

"That's it," Draven told him. "It's just us in here. You don't have to fight—there's nothing to fight against. Now tell me where you are."

Ash was silent for long moments, but then his head fell back against the hollow of Draven's shoulder, baring his throat as all remaining tension drained out of him at once.

"With you," he said in a hoarse whisper. "I'm on Terra Nova… with you."

Draven had to swallow a couple of times against the thickness clogging his throat before he could reply. He supported Ash against him, the human's torso draped against his front in a graceful arch. "I'm here," he said. "I've got you. I won't let go."

"I know," Ash said, his voice distant now, rather than panicked.

"We can just sit like this until my knot goes down," Draven said. "Try to stay relaxed. It's been a while already; it shouldn't be too much longer."

But Ash shook his head, rolling it back and forth against Draven's shoulder. "No..." Still in that detached voice. "Touch me, Draven. Please. Make me come because I asked you to, not because I can't physically stop it from happening."

The words slurred a bit in places, and Draven didn't really like the way Ash sounded right now— but at least it was better than panic.

"You tell me to stop if I do something wrong," he insisted. "Say it back to me, Ash. I'm not kidding."

"I'll tell you to stop," Ash whispered.

So... Draven touched him, sliding his hands over Ash's chest as if he could somehow draw out everything bad that had happened to him through his skin. He stroked his palms over the human's nipples until they hardened to points, and teased those points between his fingers, tugging and rolling them. Ash continued to splay himself against Draven's body like an offering, one of his arms coming up to anchor himself in place with a hand grasping the nape of Draven's neck.

Cautiously, Draven let himself explore. Ash remained pliant and open, his only reaction the occasional flutter or squeeze around the base of Draven's cock where they were joined together. Draven cupped the wrinkled velvet skin of Ash's odd human scrotum, rolling the two delicate stones inside until Ash let out a slow sigh and sank impossibly further against Draven's body.

Enough time had passed that Ash's cock showed renewed signs of life after his earlier orgasm, so Draven let his fingers close around it, sliding and squeezing until it thickened inside his grip. With his other hand, he returned to plucking and pinching one of the human's nipples.

"You're so beautiful like this, Ash," he murmured against the shell of the human's ear. "I want to watch you let go and come for me again. I want to see you lying here safe and trusting in my arms, undone with the pleasure I can give you."

Draven fisted the hard length in his hand, and Ash started to pant. His inner muscles clenched and released, clenched and released around Draven's cock, over and over—sending new waves of mating hormones rushing through Draven's veins like heady wine. Slowly, he built Ash's pleasure higher, never letting up even though his rhythm remained lazy and deliberate.

The only warning he had was the twitch and squeeze of Ash's fingers against the back of his neck, and suddenly Ash was coming hard, spilling over Draven's hand and clamping around his knot with a strangled groan. The human's chest jerked in time with his twitching cock... and kept jerking even after the rest of his body stilled.

With a sharp ache, Draven recognized the rhythmic hitch for what it was, and quickly wiped his hand clean on the sheets next to him so he could wrap both arms around Ash's chest as the human collapsed into silent weeping.

"Still got you," he promised, nuzzling against the smooth silk of Ash's hair... holding him close. "Not going anywhere. Not ever again."

He cradled Ash against his body, whispering words of love and comfort as the human finally succumbed to everything he'd been holding inside over these long, terrible months. And for the first time in his life, Draven truly understood what it was to be mated—to hold in your arms the unvarnished truth of another person, freely given and received. When his knot eventually went down, he eased both of them onto their sides with carefully controlled strength, arranging them to lie spooned together; Ash's head pillowed on his bicep and their bodies pressed close.

"Where are you now, Ash?" he asked softly, just to be sure.

"I'm with you," Ash breathed, without an instant's hesitation.

<hr>

Two days later, Draven walked with Ash toward a modest two-story home set in the suburbs of a mid-sized city about five hundred kilometers south of New Brussels. The engine compartment of the rented hovercar behind them ticked and hissed quietly as it cooled in the pleasant afternoon breeze.

All of them had been debriefed by the Terra Novan authorities, as well as by Ambassador Martinez herself. Law enforcement seemed content with the information they'd been given—that Ilarius was in chaos, Ash had been illegally taken as a slave by a high-ranking Vithii in the Regime, and Draven and Kade had acted to free him before his master killed him. It also didn't hurt that the Adjunct's official cause of death had come back as suffocation due to airway swelling, secondary to a bee sting.

As far as anyone else was concerned, Ash had been an unarmed, physically weaker human fighting for his life against a Vithii who'd already killed half a dozen *veelaht*s over the years. Only the bizarre stroke of luck of a bee getting into the house and stinging the Adjunct as they fought had allowed Ash to escape with his life. Jontalyss even confirmed that other bees had gotten into the house previously.

Of course, Draven and Kade knew better. Their delicate-looking human ally was about as harmless as a hunting predator, and the Adjunct hadn't stood a chance once Ash had decided he needed to die. Neither had the guards that he and Draven killed 'in self-defense,' when they tried to prevent Ash, Draven, and Jontalyss from leaving the house where they'd been unlawfully held prisoner.

And so, they'd been released from house arrest, and were free to travel as long as they didn't remove the non-invasive location transmitters they were wearing on their wrists. Ash had asked Draven to accompany him to this pleasant neighborhood in the suburbs for a personal visit to people he hadn't seen in far too long. Draven had immediately agreed.

The human was dressed in the same suit that had decorated the floor of Draven's bedroom a couple of nights previously—though it had since been cleaned and pressed. Somehow, Draven couldn't muster all that much surprise in response to the realization that Ash was a fashion fanatic when he wasn't neck deep in intrigue… as he had been for most of the time Draven had known him.

'Appearances are important, Draven,' Ash had pointed out dryly. *'You and I both have more cause to understand that than most.'*

And it wasn't as though Draven could argue the point. Besides, Ash looked mouth-wateringly good in the latest human male fashion, so what possible reason would he have to complain?

"Nervous?" Draven asked, casting a sideways glance at him as they walked.

Ash's eyes cut to his. "Hmm. Let's see. The last time I saw my parents, I cursed them up one side and down the other for not letting me do more to protect Shaima from Kovak's goons. Then I shoved them onto a third-class transport ship bound for Terra Nova and warned them never to try and contact me again, unless they wanted to end up with two dead children instead of one. Why would I possibly be nervous?"

Draven affected a wide-eyed expression of surprise. "*You,* Ash? Pushing people away when times are the hardest? Say it isn't so—I am *shocked* over here."

Chiseled features twisted in irritation. "You know, your gently chiding sense of humor has always been one of the things I loved most about you. Oh, hang on a minute. Did I say *'loved'*? No, I'm wrong. Not *loved*. The other thing."

Draven grinned at him, showing teeth. Then, he glanced around the quiet neighborhood, so unlike the dingy, smog-enshrouded Capital on Ilarius. Here, no one was hiding in the shadows, ready to jump out and attack them at any moment. No one cared that they were a human and a Vithii walking together. And most importantly, no one gave a damn that they were two males fucking, or that they loved each other.

So Draven reached out and snagged Ash by the arm, pulling him to a halt and turning him so they were facing each other. That made it much easier to reach down and cup his face, pulling him into a brief, heartfelt kiss.

"They're going to be thrilled to see you," he said into their shared air.

Ash took an unsteady breath and swallowed convulsively. "Thank you," he whispered.

Draven made a dismissive noise. "Oh, stop with that shite. They will be. You'll see." He quirked an eyebrow. "Though I still think you're an idiot for not calling ahead. What if they're out?"

"Then we'll wait," Ash murmured. "As long as it takes."

Draven glanced around the pleasant surroundings. "Nice day for it, at least. Now come on. Stop dragging your damned feet."

Ash huffed at him and resumed his dramatic death march toward the cheerful, red-painted door. Draven hung back a few steps as the human squared his shoulders and knocked. He held his breath, waiting to see if anyone would answer, and let it out in a slow sigh of satisfaction when the door creaked open to reveal a plump, middle-aged woman with close-cropped iron gray hair, and Ash's eyes.

"Yes, can I help you—" She cut herself off abruptly, that familiar-looking dark gaze going wide.

"Hello, Mum," Ash said quietly.

Her mouth opened, a sheen of moisture shining across her eyes. "… Ash? Is it… really you?" She blinked several times. "How… why…" Then she seemed to come back to herself, and turned back to the interior of the house. "Ibrahim! *Ibrahim! Come quickly!*"

Draven hid a smile as Ash's mother nearly fell into her son's arms, hugging him tightly and bursting into tears. Ash leaned down and buried his face against her neck, hugging her back just as hard.

Footsteps approached from inside. "What is it, Rahmi—what's wrong?" asked a tall man with long white hair, and a familiar stubborn tilt to his jaw.

Ash pulled away just far enough to meet the newcomer's eyes over his mother's shoulder. "Father," he said unsteadily, his voice sounding suspiciously choked up. "I'm… I came home."

Ash's father let out a sharp breath as though he'd been punched. A moment later, Ash was sandwiched between two sets of arms, all three of them crying unashamedly. And Draven absolutely did *not* have to blink rapidly, or press his lips together in a thin line to keep the bottom one from trembling—just a little—as he watched them.

When the little family finally broke apart, Ash's father was still looking at his son with something like amazement. "Ash… by all the gods and prophets, what are you doing here? Are you all right? What's happened?"

A moment later, the man finally seemed to realize that there was a hulking Vithii stranger hovering a few steps away from the edge of his front porch. Ash followed his gaze, and for an instant, a watery smile transformed his sharply drawn features into a portrait of radiance. He turned back to his parents.

"There's so much I have to tell you," he said, his voice unsteady with everything that had happened, and everything yet to be said. "But first, there's someone important I need you both to meet."

EPILOGUE

Ambassador Martinez tapped her stylus rhythmically against the surface of the conference table—the noise grating on Kade's overstretched nerves. The other Terra Novan officials were leaving now, after yet another endless meeting spent in fruitless debate over policy and treaty provisions. When Kade had risen to follow them, though, Isadora Martinez looked up at him and uttered a single word.

"Stay."

So he'd slowly sat back down, keeping his eyes on her as the rest of the people in the room filed out, talking amongst themselves in quiet voices. He continued to watch her face, forcing himself not to give the damned tapping stylus a pointed glare. The door slid shut behind the last straggler, and the stylus stilled its maddening rhythm.

Martinez turned her attention to the terminal set in the center of the huge table and addressed it. "Computer. Cease all recording."

The terminal beeped an acknowledgement. Kade raised an eyebrow.

"Something you wished to discuss off the record, Ambassador?" he asked, knowing his tone sounded less than welcoming.

Martinez leaned back in her chair, regarding him with a penetrating gaze. She was a striking woman, for a human—tall for her species, with caramel skin, dark brown hair, and intelligent eyes that glinted with green highlights when she was roused. She was, Kade had quickly discovered, also a shrewd negotiator. No doubt such a skill was as valuable for a diplomat as it was for a business-man, though hers was wrapped in an additional facade of charm that Kade neither possessed, nor aspired to.

"I've been talking more with Jontalyss," said the ambassador. "I've also spoken to your com-rades. Having done so, I'm guessing you're the one who put the fear of the gods into that poor girl."

Kade leaned back, matching her posture and ignoring the warning crawl of incipient neurotonin withdrawal itching at his brain.

"I'm not certain what you mean, Ambassador," he said. "Speak plainly."

Martinez's hazel eyes didn't waver. "I've known Joni for a very long time. Since our university days, right up until her bondmate started cutting her off from her friends and family about a year-and-a-half ago. Classic abusive narcissist, that one—I tried to steer her away, for all the good it did. But the point is… I know her. And *no way* did that woman help mastermind a daring escape plan from Ilarius using bee venom and a freighter shipment of *chik'taap* lumber. You and your comrades kidnapped her, just like the Ilarian authorities claimed you did."

Kade only looked at her coolly, not a muscle betraying him. He allowed the silence to stretch, waiting to see what direction she intended to take this. She held out for nearly a minute before settling her shoulders with a small sigh.

"Don't worry, though," she said. "She's sticking to her story. I think she realizes that there's no go-ing back for her now."

"Have you discussed her options, going forward?" Kade asked conversationally, even as the itching at the back of his mind grew a bit more insistent.

Martinez shrugged a shoulder. "I've suggested she seek refuge on Vithara for now. If nothing else, they have some promising new therapies related to the treatment of mating withdrawal. I know that's a big concern for her."

Kade had to swallow his snort of disdain, thinking of Ryder and all the shit she'd gone through since her bondmate's long-ago betrayal.

"I'm sure that must a big relief for her," he said evenly.

The human started twirling the stylus through her fingers, still examining him attentively. "There's been quite a boom in the medical industry on Vithara in recent years, as it happens. Including some new work related to neurotransmitter imbalances."

Irritation flared hot, though Kade knew from long and bitter experience that it was just the chemicals in his brain demanding their due. There was nothing like the realization that your identity as a sentient being was little more than a cocktail of random molecules swirling together to bring on an existential crisis... but it was an existential crisis he'd been dealing with for years now.

"I'm well aware," he said, keeping most of the irritation out of his tone. "Despite the general shitshow on display, we do, in fact, still have access to scientific journals on Ilarius."

Practicality had made it necessary for Kade to disclose his medical condition immediately after their arrest on the freighter, or risk a messy and painful death a few cycles later when his neurotonin levels crashed. But that didn't mean he'd been happy about it. And it appeared the ambassador wasn't ready to let it go quite yet.

"It's quite possible they could help you better control your... condition," she said delicately.

"Yes, it's quite possible that they could," Kade shot back. "But my jacked-up brain chemistry is hardly our primary concern right now." Though judging by the faint tremor starting in his hands, it would shortly need to become his primary concern—at least long enough to visit the building's dispensary and get his next fix.

Martinez sobered. "No. I suppose it's not."

"So...?" he prompted, in hopes of moving things along.

She tilted her head, assessing. "All right, then. Plain talk. I've been concerned about the situation on Ilarius for some time now, and I'm far from alone in that. The information you and your comrades have delivered to us isn't exactly breaking news. However, there hasn't been a mandate for interventionism within the other local systems before now."

"We've noticed," Kade told her flatly.

She nodded. "I'm sure. At any rate, whether you're willing to admit to the circumstances surrounding it or not, your delivery of someone with access to the inner circles of the Ilarian Regime—specifically, someone willing to testify about what she knows—adds additional pressure on the allied worlds to act."

"And will they?" Kade asked. "Act?"

"I suspect you're well acquainted with the slow grind of bureaucracy's wheels," she said dryly. "Though you may be interested to hear that my office has also been contacted by an official within the Maelfian Diplomatic Corps recently."

Kade perked up at the indirect news about Pax and Nahleene. "Oh? Have they now? Goodness, what are the odds…?"

A small snort escaped her. "Well, I suppose that answers one of my questions. It seems you and your friends *have* been busy lately, haven't you?"

"Yes," he agreed. "We've been very busy— trying to stay alive… trying to stay out of Regime custody… trying to prevent genocide by a psychotic dictator…"

Her expression turned grim. "Quite." She shifted in her chair, leaning forward. "Here's the thing. Getting Vithara, in particular, to give two shits about Ilarius is a hard sell. As far as they're concerned, the Vithii who fled Vithara for Ilarius after the civil war are merely returning to form. Once a bunch of war criminals, always a bunch of war criminals, right?"

"That civil war happened well over a century ago," Kade said. "Everyone involved is long dead. Unless you'd like to argue that the sins of the fathers are visited upon the sons, even unto the third and fourth generation?"

She arched a dark brow. "You'd have to tell me the answer to that, Ehkadian *Finisterre*. That's certainly a family name with a fair amount of blood attached to it in the Vitharan history books."

Kade went very still.

"And yet, my parents were the ones whose blood was spilled when they dared to stand on the wrong side of the political landscape," he said eventually.

Her eyes bored into his. "Yes," she replied. "I've done a bit of digging into your background, as it happens. It's true that Jontalyss' testimony will be helpful. So will Mr. Purandhri's—especially here on Terra Nova, with his parents being naturalized citizens. But you… your recent history is, shall we say, checkered. And yet, you would appear to be my best bet for making headway in this matter. You know how to play the game of politics, even though you clearly have contempt for it. Jontalyss and your friend—Draven, I believe his name is? They don't."

"No," Kade agreed. "You're quite right about that—they don't."

Martinez nodded. "So you see my dilemma. Do I rely on an addict with a history of shady business dealings and a family name synonymous with the phrase 'war criminal'?"

Kade felt his expression turn jaded. "Do you have a choice?"

The ambassador watched him, unblinking. "I'm still deciding that." Her eyes tracked down to his hands. "But I should let you go now. I get the impression you have other places to be. We'll talk again soon."

Kade wrapped his shaking hands around the table edge and rose, holding back the gnawing ache of withdrawal with an iron will honed by long years of practice.

"As you say," he told her. "Though, you should also know that I still have dear friends risking their lives on Ilarius. For that reason, I look forward to the day when talk stops being *talk*, and becomes *action*."

With that, he turned on his heel and left the room. The door slid shut behind him, cutting him off from the figure inside—a woman who held the future of his world in her well-manicured hands.

finis

The *Love and War* series concludes with Book 5: *Antagonist,* coming October 2019.

To discover more books by this author, visit
www.rasteffan.com